IMPASSE

IMPASSE

MICHAEL DIAMOND

ISBN: 1517704375
ISBN 13: 9781517704377
Library of Congress Control Number: 2015916621
CreateSpace Independent Publishing Platform
North Charleston, South Carolina

Chapter 1

At 10:03 a.m. on Wednesday, October 23, 2013 the call came. Anne Whalen was walking through the halls toward her office after teaching a class when her cell phone rang. "I never imagined," Alan Selden said excitedly. "I just never imagined. Anne, you won't believe what the Presiding Judge said about the case at the beginning of the Court session."

"Was Hershel found guilty?" she asked. There had been some static in the connection. She repeated, "Alan, was your uncle found guilty?"

"You have to read it for yourself. It's being posted as we speak."

"And Hershel, how is he?"

"I would say he's exhausted and exhilarated, in equal parts. Right now, he's going over the opinion with Steiner. The lawyers in the case were given an advance copy early this morning. Hershel asked me to call you so you could start reading it right away."

"Tell him I love him. No. More than that. Let him know I hold him in the highest esteem."

"I will. You know he was lucky."

"How so?"

"You were there for him."

As she walked toward her office, Anne thought about the media and the internet coverage of the case. Now there would be more, so much more, whichever way the verdict went. Reaching the door, Anne fumbled with keys and rushed to the computer on her desk. Speed-reading through the pages, she repeated aloud, several times, "Oh Lord" and "My God."

"Yes," she said to the screen, crying. "You got what you wanted and so much more, so very much more."

Hershel called in the afternoon. They talked about ramifications of the decision. "Only one thing is certain," he said, "there will be changes. Big changes." His voice, suddenly overcome by the strain of lengthy efforts, had become thinner and took on a slightly higher pitch.

Neither of them spoke for a time. Instead, they shared a quiet understanding of all they'd been through in the six years since the bombing.

"And all you ever wanted out of this," Anne said half crying and half laughing, "was punishment. You're a strange man, Hershel Selden."

"Everything that's happened is strange," he replied laughing. "And by the way, some reporters who were here when you testified want to be in touch with you. I gave them your number at the school."

"That's fine," she said. "You'll let me know if anything else is going on there? I fear that there's likely to be a backlash that..."

"No, the worst is over. I love you."

"And I love you back," Anne said, crying softly.

Later that afternoon, she began preparing herself for questions that the reporters might ask. She owed it to Hershel to get the details right, to remember the key events exactly as they happened.

"History," she said softly to herself. She'd been teaching it at Rutgers for more than thirty years. Over that period of time, she always considered it was made by a few major players, some of whom were heroes and many more who were fiends. In Hershel's case, however, there were no larger-than-life characters. History was being made by ordinary people who were just trying to figure out the right thing to do.

Anne remembered meeting Marion, Alan Selden's wife, in the fall of 2005. Marion had just begun as an adjunct professor. The two of them connected instantly and were the closest of friends. Anne became Aunt Annie to Marion's granddaughter Amy, age six, and her grandson Kevin, age eight.

Her own marriage had been brief and childless. Edward simply went on with his life elsewhere, as though vows in church were nothing more than a temporary allegiance to a certain brand of cigarettes. Anne took back her maiden name, got on with her career, and stopped thinking about having a family. She had no nephews or nieces of her own. The spirit of her only sibling, Matthew, visited her while she was sleeping at the exact moment of his death in Vietnam. The message she was to carry to their parents was that he was at peace. They were not to worry.

Then came that awful day, April 10, 2007. "May the Lord have mercy," she said softly. Anne remembered walking in the Student Union Building, past a television screen. "Among the dead," a news reporter said, "were Marion Selden, her daughter Susan, son-in-law William Warner, and two grandchildren, Kevin and Amy Warner." A photograph of Marion appeared. Anne's knees gave way. From the floor, amid the books and papers she was carrying, she looked at the screen and saw a small bus that was totally blackened. The reporter's voice said something about a "suicide bomber" and "a blast that shattered windows in this small town on the outskirts of Jerusalem." As the programming returned, in mid-sentence, to an afternoon soap opera, her mind began drifting away.

She felt strong hands of students picking her up and gently lowering her into an oversized leather chair. Tears and the presence of apparitions obliterated the urgent callings and scurryings that would bring a nurse.

"I won't keep them long," she remembered saying to a presence that she knew was the Jesus to whom she prayed her whole life. He nodded. With that, Marion appeared. Anne caressed her face with both hands. Then she hugged Marion's daughter, Judith and Judith's husband, Bill. "So sorry. So sorry," she said as Kevin and Amy bounded toward her. Anne sat on her haunches, and the children, as they always did, bowled her over, laughing. "You're about to have an adventure," she said, beaming at them. Kevin, age ten, looking exactly like his father, said "I know." "And me too," said Amy, age eight, eagerly. "It's not just for boys," she added emphatically. "I do trust," Anne responded, "you two will remember that I love you and always will. Your weird Aunt Annie loves you up to..." "We know," Kevin and Amy said, one after the other, as if the question was too stupid to deserve a response.

A nurse who had come from her office in the Student Union Building leaned down toward Anne's face and asked her who she was and where she was.

"Later," she told the nurse, and yelled "Up to the outside sky," toward Kevin and Amy, as they slipped away. She listened carefully for a moment, thinking they might return, hoping that Amy would come up from behind her, tap her on the shoulder, and share a little secret the way she often did, woman-to-woman.

The television screen went on to sell trips to Disneyland. Nearby, students jostled one another. A blood pressure cuff was taken off Anne's arm. She remembered walking away slowly, as though surveying the extent of her property remaining, following the storm that swept Marion and the children out of her life.

Anne remembered how she and Marion would often walk the campus together. She was taller than Marion with Celtic pale skin, blue eyes, and long grey hair that had the last vestiges of red. Marion was olive in color. Her hair was shiny black, and her eyes were dark. Anne's facial expressions came to rest in a drawn look of concern. Marion's face rested in a dimpled smile, punctuated by the hint of care-lines at the corners of her eyes.

Anne remembered, as if it were yesterday, them sitting on a bench outside the dining hall. Warm November winds were lightly settling fallen leaves onto the carpeting of campus grass. Anne warned Marion not to take her new academic career too seriously.

"Coming from you, that's sad to hear."

"Nevertheless true," Anne said. "No one believed more than I did that teaching history would be of some social benefit."

"Haven't some of your students used lessons from the past? None of them became lawyers like Louis Brandeis or doctors with a mission, like Albert Schweitzer?"

"I see no evidence of that, not even close."

Marion put a hand on Anne's shoulder and smiled. "You can't be seeing to the end of all their careers. You're good, Anne Whalen," she said, "but you're not that good."

"Lately, my students are interested in getting ahead and precious little else," Anne said sadly. "Civic efforts got lost somewhere. Sometimes I think that real truths haven't the slightest chance of surfacing in these United States of S.A.P."

"S.A.P." Marion said, laughing. "What the hell is S.A.P.?"

"Stupidity, amnesia, and propaganda. You'll see," Anne remembered saying, as an updraft caused leaves to swirl around them. "Expecting this crop of American students to grasp their history and use it to change beliefs and behaviors is like expecting that these leaves will somehow blow back up into the trees, attach themselves from where they had loosened, and turn green again."

Anne remembered the two of them walking back toward their offices that day. She recalled how kind Marion had been. Sensing that Anne's sadness was deepening, Marion held Anne's hand the whole way. By the time they had reached their destination, both of them smiled at one another, and Anne remembered having received the blessing of deep friendship from Marion Selden on that warm November afternoon.

Chapter 2

She remembered when she met first Alan Selden. It was in December of 2005. Marion had invited her to their home in Westfield for dinner. Alan was in his sixties, but looked a good deal younger. Taller than Marion, with fairer skin, blue eyes, and thinning blond hair, he had the rugged, square-jawed look of a movie star who was aging splendidly.

Much of dinner conversation had to do with their daughter Judith, her husband Bill, and the two grandchildren, Kevin and Amy. Judith, Anne remembered being told, was a grade school teacher. Bill was an accountant. "And the kids," Marion said, "there's no describing the kids. You'll just have to meet them."

"I quite agree," Alan added quickly.

After dinner, Marion suggested that they relax in Alan's study while she did the dishes. Alan led Anne into a large room with a picture window facing the back yard. A light snow was brushing against the pane. A dark wooden desk with comfortable-looking leather chairs were in front of the window. The short wall spaces to the left and right of the window and the walls to the left and right of the desk were filled with bookshelves. The wall opposite the desk was covered with pictures. Anne walked toward them. Pictures, she remembered, were a great way to get to know someone.

Her father, Thomas Whalen, long gone, taught her such things when she was a youngster. He called them part of interviewing skills. She'd come home one day and proudly announced that a girl she met at a friend's party, Susan was her name, "was going straight to hell because she didn't get baptized in the Lord."

Her father explained that the nuns who taught at her school were wrong about some things, one of which was that God would never punish a good person. To do so would be evil. She recalled that he used that word, evil. Her homework was to ask Susan all the questions she could think of to find out if Susan might have done anything wrong in her life, or whether she was thinking about stealing anything or hurting someone.

Several days later, Anne told her father about the questions she'd asked and what Susan's answers were. That gentle prodding by her father encouraged Anne to steer her Christianity away from the shoals of a stilted Catholicism and toward an all encompassing religion, based on the teachings of Christ as she would come to understand them.

Anne carried a note home from school one day. Sister Evelyn had reacted with fury. Her parents were required to meet with the Sister concerning "a serious breach of doctrinal truths." Anne's mother read the note and frowned. That night, her parents had, what she remembered was, a long quiet conversation. Their meeting with Sister Evelyn passed without comment in the house, but the next year, Anne and her brother were enrolled in the public school system of Manchester, New Hampshire.

"Football?" she asked, looking at a picture of players in uniform seated on steps in the front of a gymnasium. Heavier players, the linemen, were up front. Alan was in the second row. She guessed he had been a halfback.

"Just waiting for the New York Giants to call," he responded, nodding at the telephone on his desk. "Should be any time now." There was a theatrical, practiced quality to his answer. Alan had obviously delivered that line many times before.

The next picture that captured her gaze was a side view of Alan, in the open air with trees in the background, aiming a revolver. "Should I be worried?" she asked, laughing.

"Not at all. My first job out of law school was an Assistant County Prosecutor. The law allowed us to carry firearms. That being the case, the Prosecutor required all of us to take a short basic course in how to use a gun. So, that's me before I missed the side of a barn." Again, the answer was well-delivered. If the opportunity presented itself, she would ask Alan if he ever acted.

Anne quickly gazed across more than a dozen items, including a photo with Alan and New Jersey Governor Jon Corzine, a Kiwanis Club award, a Chamber of Commerce plaque, a Muhlenberg College Debating Society award, and a Seton Hall Law School Alumni Citation. Okay, she said to herself, question answered. The acting part of Alan's behavior would have been enhanced, if not begun, from his being a college debater and then a lawyer.

After looking closely at a picture of men and women wearing t-shirts with lettering that she couldn't quite make out, Alan told her about the Selden Slammers, a softball team made up of employees and former employees of his law firm.

When she got to an award from the Bnai Brith, Anne tried pronouncing the first word. Alan corrected her. She asked him what it meant. "Sons of the Covenant," he said. "It started as a service organization sometime around 1840, to help Jewish immigrants make a new life and take care of things like hospital and burial costs."

"Something like the Ancient Order of Hibernians," she responded, "helping..."

"Something like that," he interrupted.

Anne took note of Alan being an interrupter. That was a common malady in America of the twenty-first century. More and more people had become interrupters, perhaps, she thought, owing to the easy ability to change television channels and radio stations, skip email messages, and turn away from streaming internet information. No longer was one required to endure, even for a millisecond, data that did not accord favorably with one's own thoughts and predilections.

They moved into chairs in the study. Anne turned her attention to the wall of bookshelves to her left. "Law books?" she asked.

"They're my orphans," he responded.

Anne laughed. "How sad," she said. "You mean they're no longer being distributed?"

"Correct. Even law libraries have become rows of computer cubby holes where guys look at screens instead of books piled up. The changeover was hard for me. I was approaching my sixties, and all of a sudden I had to use search terms instead of an old fashioned index."

"Alan, you do not at all look like a man in his sixties."

"Thank you. I'm sixty, to be exact."

"And I just became seventy last month, to be exact. The changeover to computer searching was a little difficult for me also. But now, I wouldn't be without it. There's ever so much more information available to us researchers than ever before. Except..."

"Except what?"

"Well, the information is like a river that flows so much faster now. You can get washed downstream quickly. There used to be quiet little coves where one could tie up in and ponder items of information as they slowly became available. No more. Now, with the click of a mouse, the coves are inundated. I'm spending more time now determining the line between useful and over-the-top information." Anne was impressed that Alan had listened to that fairly extended answer. She concluded that he was a nominal, and not an inveterate, interrupter.

Anne walked to the opposite wall where there was another collection of books. Those were not law books. They were personal choices and gifts from people who knew Alan and Marion. One section contained the typical novels about spies, mysteries, and thrillers. "You're a fan of Graham Greene?" she asked.

"Sure, and Grishom and le Carre."

Another grouping of books included *Diary of a Young Girl* by Anne Frank, *Exodus* by Leon Uris, *Inside the Third Reich* by Albert Speer, and a copy of the play, *Judgment at Nuremberg* by Abby Mann.

"My mother and father, Ellen and Thomas, were saints," Anne said, turning to Alan. "When I repeated what the nuns told me about only believers in Jesus being saved, they said that all good people, no matter what their faith or their shadings of belief might be, would be given the best of treatment in the next world."

"Never met them, but I like your folks."

"Are you one of the good people who can expect the best in the next encounter? My dad liked it when I asked that question."

Alan laughed and then sat back in his chair, gazing at the ceiling. "Interesting question." After a short while he asked, "Are you quite certain there's an afterlife?"

"Yes, without a doubt. But I won't bore you with the evidence right now. So, your answer. Are you one of the good people?"

"I stole one thing in my life."

"What was that?"

"A book. I read it and never stole anything else in my whole life. Stealing that book scared the shit out of me. It was as though the event had been scripted to keep me on the right path."

"So, you stole a bible. New or Old Testament?"

"Neither," said Alan. "It was *Les Misérables*. I took it as a message. Couldn't have been any plainer. So," he chuckled, "I never stole so much as a postage stamp, and I never hurt anyone in my life. Has that question been answered to your satisfaction?"

"My father would have been proud of you."

She had just asked Alan if he enjoyed the practice of law when Marion came into the study to announce an end to shoptalk. Coffee and dessert were on the table.

Sitting at the table, Alan answered the question. He'd found it a relatively easy life, not much more arduous than debating on behalf of whichever side would pay the bill. "Just day-to-day living and putting bread on the table. We're not all like Moses coming down from the mountain as lawgivers."

"And the law," Anne responded, "is like rules of the road in a well ordered society."

"Yes. Perfectly stated," he replied.

Anne raised her cup. "To lawyers." They all laughed. "And may the Selden Slammers softball team never lose a game."

"That's too much to hope for," Marion said. "I've seen them play. It ain't pretty."

Chapter 3

The thought of never seeing Marion's grandchildren again was painful for Anne. All the caskets remained closed throughout the memorial service and the burial ceremony that followed. She remembered asking Alan that morning if there might be a viewing. He shook his head no, saying "It's better that way." She especially wanted to see the faces of the children for one last time, perhaps to catch an inkling of the trajectories that their lives might have taken.

Kevin was a quiet child, eight years old when she first met him. He went along with playing softball and being athletic. That was no challenge, but it was unlikely that sports would have been the center of his life. The boy's focus was elsewhere.

One day, Anne saw him sitting quietly in a chair that was pulled up to Marion's kitchen counter where she had created a windowsill garden. He was looking at a small aloe plant. As she got closer, Anne noticed that he was looking intently at a particular shoot of the small plant. Next to that shoot was a clear plastic drink stirrer. It had been placed into the soil immediately adjacent to the shoot and stood at the exact angle that the shoot was growing. There was a spot of white paint on the plastic stirrer about a half-inch lower than the height of the shoot. Kevin had been keeping track of the rate of growth of that aloe plant.

"Is it a school project?" she asked.

"No," he answered, still looking at the stick and the shoot.

"Is the plant okay?"

"Yes, but how does it know when to stop? I mean Grammy has another one like this that's been the same for a long time."

"I wish I knew," she responded. "Kevin, when you begin to figure that out, would you let me know? It's a great question. I never gave it much thought."

Kevin nodded and went back to observing and measuring the aloe plant.

Anne imagined the bomb going off in the bus. Did Kevin, the consummate young observer, give a short bit of critical thought to the compression he felt in his facial muscles? And when the orderly thinking process of the outer cortical layer of his brain began to give way just after the first impact, was he nevertheless able to make judgments about the torrents of feelings and fears that came rushing up out of his primitive limbic system below? Anne imagined that he'd been able to do that. She pictured him as being an intrepid observer to the end of life and into the realms that lie beyond ours.

She often cried when she thought about the children. They were in her dreams. On occasion, when she most felt the need for being comforted, Anne saw herself entering a quiet waiting room adjacent to the sacred space they now occupied. It was a warm place, flooded with light and undulating waves of love. Amy and Kevin would come into the room, and the three of them would talk quietly, holding hands.

Amy was six years old when Anne first met her. Marion had asked if her granddaughter could sit in her office while she was meeting privately with a student. While Anne was in the middle of a series of telephone calls, Marion piled several cushions and a few large books onto the seat of a chair at a conference table near Anne's desk. After helping Amy into the chair, she put a legal pad and cup filled with sharpened pencils in front of the girl. The cup had the faint outlines of the international radioactive trefoil symbol. Bold lettering over that symbol read, "Use With Care. Words Can Kill."

Amy's back was to Anne. She watched as the girl carefully took one pencil out of the cup and started writing something on the pad. Certain that Amy was safely occupied, Anne continued with her telephone calls.

A short time later, Anne got up to retrieve a note which had a student's telephone number out of her handbag. The handbag was on the table. Standing over Amy, she reached for the bag and froze in place. The child was drawing the handbag, and the drawing was like no other she had ever seen a youngster make.

The bag was large and tan. It was lying on its side, with a sizable depiction of Kokopelli, the fertility deity usually seen as a humpbacked flute player, facing up to the ceiling. The long leather strap was curled upon itself. The girl was in the process of drawing the pocketbook in three dimensions. She showed the depth of it by shading the underside with a series of light curved lines. Amazingly, Amy knew to make the farther end smaller than the one closest to her. Was the girl imagining perspective lines to some vanishing point? And her Kokopelli, a near exact replica, was, in fact, drawn lying on its side, facing the ceiling. The curled leather strap was shown to gradually go from its full width to being upright as it slowly wound several times upon itself. Those techniques were well beyond the usual skills of a six year old. Anne slowly, without saying a word, retreated back to her desk while Amy kept drawing.

When it appeared as though the girl had finished, Anne went to retrieve her pocketbook. Missing a front tooth and smiling, Amy looked up and said, "There. There's your pocketbook."

"And the most beautiful picture of my pocketbook ever made," Anne told her.

"You know what you just became?"

"What," the girl asked, laughing.

"My favorite artist. That's what."

Later that day, Anne showed Marion the drawing that Amy had done. "I know," said Marion.

"How is that possible?"

"A gift. That's the way it was described to Susan and Bill. Some children are born with abilities beyond their years."

"I don't mean to intrude, but are they putting her into some stepped-up program where the girl's full talents can be realized?"

"Her parents got professional advice on that score. They were told it would be best to hold off with special schooling unless Amy exhibited a strong compulsion for artistic excellence. She's better off having a full childhood, in the local school with all the experiences that come with growing up."

"It's just so amazing," Anne said looking at the picture.

"So, if and when Amy, herself, feels the need for more contact with fine arts teachers, we'll certainly help Bill and Susan bring that off. For now, Amy is best off just being a great little kid, who's learning all she can about the world around her."

Chapter 4

Anne Whelan recalled when she first met Hershel Selden. It was in the spring of 2006, a year before the suicide bombing. At the time, he lived in Jerusalem with his wife, Sarah. Their two sons, Nathan and Levi, resided nearby, and the grandchildren had settled in suburbs that were short distances away. Marion told Anne that Hershel was coming to the United States on business. He often came to the United States and rarely missed a chance to spend time with his nephew Alan's family.

Alan described the business that Hershel ran with Nathan and Levi as "cutting edge technology for the future of modern agriculture." They had developed sensitive gauges to assess moisture in soil and then deliver exact amounts of water to the roots of plants. It was called drip irrigation. Evaporation and runoff were minimized. The company developed and owned several key patents for the process. "While Hershel is by no means a Jacob Astor or a John D. Rockefeller," Alan said, "his business has provided him with resources for more than just the usual comfortable retirement."

Anne was helping Marion in the kitchen late that Sunday morning when they heard Kevin and Amy yell out that he was here. After washing her hands clean of cookie dough, she went into the living room. Hershel was embracing Marion, Alan, and the children. Then he sat down and took presents out of a shopping bag for Amy and Kevin.

Amy's gift was a thick quill graphite pencil attached to a drawing pad with red ribbon. After she untied the ribbon and was hefting the pencil, he read what he'd written on the top of the first page. "Dear Amy. With this pencil, when you have some time, please draw a picture of me. If it's okay with you, make me taller and handsomer than I am. Great artists like you can do things like that so easily. The critics call it artistic license. Love, Hershel."

She hugged Hershel and kissed his face. He gave Amy a long hug back, then watched the girl take the graphite quill pencil to the paper so that she could test the quality of lines produced by contact with the different parts of that ingenious drawing instrument.

Then Hershel took out a plain white box that was also tied with a red ribbon and gave it to Kevin. The boy untied the ribbon and carefully removed a small pair of binoculars with a camouflage exterior. "That's what the soldiers are given, Kevin. But I know you. You'll put it to much better uses."

Kevin let loose with a loud, long "Coooool" on his way to the living room window. "Aren't you going to say thank you?" Marion reminded him. "Oh. I'm sorry," the boy said as he rushed back to give his uncle a big straight-up man-to-man hug.

When Hershel stood up again, Anne observed that he was tall, lean, and elegant looking in his dark grey suit. She would never have guessed that he was more than ten years older than her. In his younger years, he'd been a soccer player of some renown. Alan had previously told Anne that Hershel helped coach a professional soccer team in Israel. His current workouts included interval sprinting, running up and down stairs at the stadium, and weightlifting.

Marion turning to Anne and Hershel said, "I would like you to meet a very special friend of mine. This is Anne Whalen. We work together."

"Marion has spoken of you often," Anne said.

He put out his hand. As they shook hands, he placed his left hand over Anne's. She noticed that he wore a thin gold wedding band and a complicated gold watch with a map of the world that was engineered to track a multitude of events. "I warned her to stop spreading lies." She noted that his English, with just a hint of a German accent, was perfect. His deep blue eyes accentuated a smile that warmed her. She wanted to know more about him.

"It's a pleasure to meet you," Anne said.

"So, you teach?"

"Yes, history, at a college nearby, with Marion."

"That's wonderful," he said.

"What's wonderful," Alan said to Anne, as he put an arm around Hershel's shoulders, "is that you're talking to a man who *made* history."

"Nephews are too easily impressed," Hershel said laughing.

"But what does Alan mean when he says that you made history?" she asked.

"It's an overstatement," Hershel responded. "The best way to describe it is to ask you who's the greatest boxer you know of?"

"I don't know. Joe Lewis? Muhammad Ali? Jack Dempsey? My grandfather, on July 4th, always remembered to raise a glass to the memory of Jack Dempsey and how he defeated The Giant, Jess Willard, in 1919."

"Perfect. So, take Jack Dempsey," Hershel said. "Alan looks at me like I'm ten Jack Dempseys. Ten. No less."

We arranged ourselves in the living room. Marion brought coffee and sat in a wing chair across from Hershel on the sofa. Anne sat next to him. Kevin remained at the window, observing the neighborhood with his field glasses. Amy sat on the floor, drawing, from memory, a fruit tree in bloom with a ladder standing under it. Alan brought in a dining room chair and placed it next to his uncle. He turned the chair around and leaned on the back part as he started to ask a series of questions, like a lawyer taking his favorite witness over testimony they'd both given forth many times in the past.

"Uncle, tell Anne what it was like growing up in Hitler's Germany."

"Wasn't so terrific," Hershel said, laughing. "So lunch is ready? Yes?"

"Listen, the woman sitting next to you is a respected professor of history at Rutgers University, Dr. Whalen. When you speak to her, you are communicating with her students and all those with whom those students converse. You can give this a few moments of your time."

"Alan is serious," Hershel said, smiling. "What can I do? Please stop me if I get boring. Promise?"

"I so swear," Anne told him.

Hershel folded his hands in his lap and considered what he was about to say. He then went on to describe the details of his life in Wurzburg, Germany when he was twelve years of age in 1933. His father was a physician, a cultured man who loved literature and classical music. To him, Hitler was a buffoon who would soon be driven in disgrace from the stage of German history. Hershel's mother agreed. Anti-Semitism made no sense. Hadn't her own father fought for Germany in the First World War?

"I loved going to the public school," Hershel continued, "but Jews were no longer allowed to attend. That's when I became fascinated with philosophy and especially with Spinoza."

"Baruch Spinoza?" said Anne. "You must have been quite precocious."

"Not at all."

"Then how...?"

"One of my teachers in the public school hated the Nazis, but feared criticizing them directly. So he spoke often about Spinoza's belief in the redemptive capacity of reason. Any system, he said, religious or otherwise, that was dependant upon assumptions instead of observable truths would not prove trustworthy."

"So, after you left, you continued to study Spinoza?"

"I did. It was like holding a place for myself in school."

Alan picked up the questioning. "And your parents assured you, did they not, that you'd be back in school as soon as Hitler was thrown out of office?"

"Right. Meanwhile, they did their best to help the Hebrew Teachers Seminary expand to take in all the Jewish kids who could no longer go to the public school."

But the streets of the City, Hershel went on, told a more urgent story. Thugs and young Nazis went around beating up Jews while the police looked the other way. Hershel told of how he fought back and developed a reputation for quickness and strength.

"What do you mean by that?" Alan asked, looking at Kevin still at the window with his binoculars and knowing that the boy would surely be listening. "You fought back, you said?"

"Well, I was strong and tall in those days. But there would often be a dozen of them. They could have easily..." Hershel looked at Amy and then at Kevin and stopped himself from describing what was in his mind.

"Right," Alan said. "So, for weeks they brought bigger and bigger guys to take you down. Isn't that what happened?"

"But you were the champ," Kevin said, turning away from his surveillance of cars parked and passing.

"For just a short time," said Hershel. "I knew they were about to lose patience with me and end the charade of a Jew thinking that he could contend with them."

"So, how did you get away?" Anne asked.

"The Hebrew Teachers Seminary organized a trip to Palestine. I signed up for it, and when I got there, I stayed. My new home was a kibbutz near Jerusalem."

"Cooool," said Kevin.

"But the fighting didn't stop, did it Uncle?" Alan asked.

"There was," Hershel paused, staring at the back of his hands, "resentment by many of the Arabs that we were settling in Palestine. But it was either be there or," he looked at Anne in a pleading way, "accept the Nazi solution."

"Then came 1948 and the War of Independence," said Alan, "tell Anne what you did then. C'mon Uncle, don't be shy."

"Wars are stupid," he spit back at his nephew.

"Okay," Alan said, "but you didn't shirk your duty."

"Did I say that wars are stupid? I didn't mean to leave out that they're brutal and ugly too."

"You won the War of Independence," Alan said. "The kid who started as a street fighter in Germany helped win the War of Independence for the State of Israel. You went from being treated like an animal that could be hunted down and murdered to being a citizen of a great country that's devoted to the principle that it will never, never again happen to the Jews."

Anne saw that Hershel's face reflected mixtures of pride and sadness. He seemed to be reaching for words that couldn't quite find their way to the surface. Trapped, they ground against one another, bringing on an obvious mental distress.

"There seemed to be no choice," Hershel said, trailing his words off so that "choice" was barely whispered.

The room was quiet. Hershel continued. "It was as though Spinoza had lived on the moon."

Turning to Anne, "Do you know what I mean?"

"I do. Yes," she responded.

"The witness is excused," Alan said triumphantly.

Chapter 5

On the day of the bombing, Anne cleared her schedule and hurried over to Marion's house. Alan was alone. She put her arms around him and drew him close to her, telling him several times how sorry she was, how very sorry. He tried to speak, but could not. She felt tremors down his chest and in his abdomen. She imagined them to be cascading shocks of loss, disbelief, and despair. Anne led Alan slowly to a couch in the living room.

The telephone rang. He made no move to answer it. She answered it in the kitchen, thanked the caller for his concern, made a note of the call, and the telephone number of the caller. Alan nodded his appreciation. Marion always kept her house key in a bowl in the front hall. She took it from the bowl and showed Alan that she was putting it in her purse. Again, he nodded his approval and managed a smile.

In the quiet, Anne brought him chamomile tea and a biscuit with strawberry preserves. He sipped the tea and took small bites of the biscuit. She answered a number of calls and talked with his friends and members of the family. They would begin arriving soon to lend their support.

She stopped by on occasion, just to make sure that he was well and to take care of a few of the many grim details. By agreement, she made arrangements with the Israeli Embassy in Washington for the release and transporting of the bodies to the United States. And Anne contacted the media to make sure they would not be a constant presence on the lawn and at the front door. She accomplished that by arranging dates and times for interviews, using the admonition that all other efforts would be met with stony, no comment reactions.

Anne continued to stop by now and then. One evening, about ten days after the tragedy, she was surprised to see Hershel. He sat in a folding chair by the window that Kevin had used to test his binoculars. Unshaven and unkempt, Anne kissed his cheek and sat next to him, holding his hand.

"It wasn't supposed to be like this," he said, staring out the window.

"What do you mean?" she said softly.

"None of us imagined," he replied, still staring out the window.

"Imagined?"

"That it could only end," looking around the room, "like this."

She had no idea what Hershel meant. She squeezed his hand gently. He took a long breath and looked over to that part of the living room where he had given Amy and Kevin their gifts. "It's my fault. I did this," he said.

Anne heard a woman's voice whispering loudly, "Stop that." It was Sarah, who'd come over with Alan to where they were sitting by the window. Sarah paid little attention to Anne. She was glaring at Hershel. Small, intense, with grey hair combed into a tight bun, "He's making no sense, my husband," she asserted.

"Yes, he's not himself," Alan said softly and suggested that the two of them go upstairs and rest. "The flight must have been long and difficult."

When Hershel and Sarah had gone, Anne asked him, "What the hell was all that about?"

Alan sat down next to Anne. "Soon after he heard about the bombing, Hershel began saying that it was all his fault. He was responsible for the deaths of his relatives and everyone else on that bus."

"How can that possibly be?"

"Hershel relates the suicide bombing to something he'd done almost sixty years before in 1948, somewhere near the same area, during the War of Independence."

"That very sweet man must be confused," she responded. "It happens quite a bit now with people his age. Can you let Sarah know that he needs to be treated gently. Delusions cannot be undone with a stick."

"I don't think she'll listen to that advice. She's angry with him. She tells him whatever happened back then was necessary. He lost his family in Germany. She lost most of hers in Germany. Where the hell were they going to go? If not Israel, where?"

"Good question," Anne said.

"But Hershel keeps mulling over what had happened in 1948, and Sarah is becoming more and more furious with him."

"I picked them up at the airport," Alan continued. "Hershel sat in the front. Sarah sat behind us. They argued, I think for my benefit, hoping that I would take sides and thereby end the deadlock."

"'So what should we have done,' she asked him, 'played nice with the Arabs and let them tattoo numbers on us, like in Europe where they made lampshades and soap out of good little Jews who walked obediently into the gas chambers? Is that what we should have done?'"

"Was that a fair comment?" Anne asked.

"She had a point," Alan responded, "and it's an opinion widely held in Israel. Do you know what some Israelis call the European Jews?"

"No idea."

"Soap. They call them soap."

"But how did Hershel respond to what Sarah said?"

"Hershel was silent for a time. Then he started talking quietly about Nazis and Arabs, almost as though he'd been thinking it through and now he was thinking out loud. We'd done no harm to the Nazis. To the Arabs we were invaders. Hitler whipped up thousands of years of anti-Semitism. Through much of that time, Arabs were our protectors. Stuff like that."

"What did Sarah say?"

"'So what!' she retorted. 'Very fancy words. So, we should have let them throw us into the sea? That's what you want for Nathan and Levi and the children?'"

"'No, of course not,'" Hershel was quick to say. "'but it's complicated.'"

"Well, Sarah didn't buy any of that complicated stuff. 'Complicated, my ass. Either you live or you die, and sometimes you have to be hard about it.'"

"Alan, did you weigh in on one side or the other?"

"Yes. I told him he should listen to his wife. I didn't know what he did that he considered so awful, but, to me he was the fighter that I wanted us to be, and there was no better time or place in the world to be a fighter. So, that's what I said.

"Then, when you came into my house, you saw him muttering that it was his fault, and you saw Sarah trying to shut him up again. That's where we are."

Anne didn't see Hershel again until days later at the funeral service for Marion, Judith, Bill, Kevin, and Amy at the Anche Emeth Temple in New Brunswick. He was sitting, head down, in the middle of the second row, next to Sarah.

The five caskets were lined up, end to end, roughly in age order, with Marion on the far left and Amy on the far right. Framed photographs of them stood upright on each coffin.

Three generations, she said to herself, shouldn't be going up at the same time. God would not have been in such a hurry. No, this was history gone wrong, yet again.

The congregation was reading prayers, alternating between Hebrew and English. When they reached the prayer known as the *Kadish*, Anne read the English description of it on the facing page. That venerated prayer for the dead, the book noted, was not in Hebrew; it was in Aramaic.

She let the words wash over her as if her soul could bathe in them and be purified. Aramaic was the language, she knew, that Christ spoke. Somewhere in the Middle East, in Syria she remembered, it was still being used, but would soon be forgotten. That saddened her. His messages had been translated into a Babel of tongues, but the core of it all, love and concern, had so obviously been disregarded. Perhaps his words needed to be understood, she thought, in the clear context of the language that he spoke, Aramaic.

Friends and family talked, through tears, glowingly about Marion, Judith, Bill, Amy, and Kevin. They would be missed, so sorely missed. And the Rabbi, a tall, bearded man in a white, fringed prayer shawl, looked up toward the domed ceiling when he said that the "ways of the Lord are beyond our understanding."

Anne also looked up, and when she did, she saw yet another aspect of how history had gone wrong. That Temple in New Brunswick reminded her of the

Alhambra Palace in Spain; it was Arabic in design. In addition to the dome, there were arches within arches and walls that were decorated with filigree designs. Repeating patterns bespoke flowers and seashells and stars in the heavens. An array of magnificent fractals reflected the beautiful complexity of the Earth. Neither Arabs nor Jews allowed representations of God, so they decorated the inner spaces of holy places with designs that bespoke the truth that God is everywhere, down to the nooks and crannies of every space. Sacred.

And then Anne remembered why Jews would so assiduously make use of Arab architecture and design. It was, in good part, a recalling of the golden era of freedom they experienced under Arab rule in Spain in the thirteenth century and in the protective Ottoman Empire thereafter. That freedom had been a respite from torrents of hatred.

Anne didn't go to the cemetery to observe the burials, and she didn't go to Alan's house where people were gathering thereafter. She went back to work, thinking she might, one day, grapple with the question of how the solid, supportive connection between Arabs and Jews had come to be abandoned, as though it never existed.

Chapter 6

Realizing she hadn't seen Alan alone in several months, Anne called to suggest they have dinner at one of his favorite Italian restaurants in Westfield. After being seated, she remembered to give him Marion's key to the front door. He hesitated as he took it and then stared at it for an unusually long time before putting it in his jacket pocket.

She sensed that Alan's world had been configured for him mainly by his family. With them gone, he was required to build the struts of his life anew, item by item. The key went from being a crucial possession that Marion carried and was so careful never to lose to being an extra piece of metal that he would now have to find a place for. Should he leave it in that bowl on the table in the front hall, the way she did every time she came through the front door? He'd find a place for it when he got home, maybe in the same bowl or in the top drawer of the tall dresser in the bedroom.

"How's the season going for your Selden Slammers?" she asked, hoping that he'd thrown himself into playing softball.

Alan hesitated before answering. "They carry my name, but that's pretty much it."

"Well, I call that the end of an era," she said with feigned sadness. "What are you doing instead?"

"Speaking."

"How does that happen? You're barely retired from softball, and you've already been made an icon and put on a speaker's tour to tell about your glorious career?"

"I wish," he said, with a slight smile. "No. I get a lot of calls to talk at organizations. I tell them about Marion, Bill, Judith, and the kids. I guess that's become my way of keeping in touch with them."

"You may not want to overdo the speaking engagements. I imagine it's hard enough to move on."

It wasn't clear that he had heard Anne. After a few spoons of soup, Alan said, "His name was Rami Abu Mussal.

The suicide bomber. Nineteen years old. Terrorist son of a bitch who didn't give a rat's ass about human life."

"Did he leave a note?"

"No."

"A recorded statement?"

"No."

"Was he connected to a terrorist group?"

"No. He was just a beast with a bomb."

"The police are satisfied with that?" Anne asked.

"Yes, but not Hershel. He hired private investigators to find out more about this Rami Abu Mussal, and he met with members of the family."

"Interesting," said Anne, "what did he find out?"

Alan shook his head and went back to eating soup. Anne decided not to follow that question up with another. The main course was served. Both of them told the waiter that they would like grated Parmesan cheese. After the waiter left the table, Alan said, "Quiet."

"What?"

"All that effort just to find out that Mussal was quiet. In the end, he wasn't so quiet, was he?"

"Not at all," Anne said, holding back from discussing what she'd learned from researching the literature on suicide bombers. They tended not to be crazed characters bent on committing deadly acts of cruelty. Most of them were well educated. Most of them were timid introverts who were reacting to conditions around them, circumstances of helplessness and humiliation. They were, she thought, in the end, observers, keen observers. And Anne wondered whether Kevin and Rami had, for even a few seconds, an opportunity to study one another and somehow find a commonality, both envisioning a better world unfolding after the blast. Are they watching us even now? Anne asked herself. Are they praying with one another that their sacrifices would turn out to have been well spent?

"Yeah, and If I were there," Alan said in a loud voice, "I would have put him in an airtight steel cage so the explosive would have torn every stinking bit of that little shit into microscopic pieces, and I would have let the pieces rot, right there in the middle of the road while all the buses passed."

The restaurant became quiet. Small talk of the day had been pushed aside by Alan's fury. The manager, a short man with a polite manner came to their table. Tilting his head slightly and cupping his hands together, as though in prayer, he said, "I'm so deeply sorry, Mr. Selden. If I could empty the restaurant for you, I would do so. But you see..."

"Sabastiano," Alan said, "I didn't mean to..."

"That's alright. We are part of your family. Please. Please allow me to bring after dinner drinks for you and your friend."

The two of them quietly sipped Drambuies. Anne asked Alan about how Hershel was doing. He savored his drink instead of responding. "The last thing I recall," Anne said, "is that he was losing his faculties and upsetting his family."

Alan laughed. "He's still doing it. They think he's crazy. I think so too."

"That poor man."

"Anne, he's telling anyone who'll listen that he killed his own family."

"And he says that because?"

"Because of what he says he did in 1948."

"Doesn't make all that much sense, does it?" Anne asked, shaking her head.

"Well, one day, he walked into a police station, demanding to be arrested for the murders of members of his family who were blown up by a suicide bomber just outside of Jerusalem. The officers questioned him. When they ascertained that he neither hired nor even knew the bomber, they declined to arrest him."

"End of story?" Anne asked.

"Hardly. The local court was next to the police department. Hershel went right up to the judge, complaining that the police refused to arrest him. Well, the judge didn't know what he was dealing with, so he called an army lieutenant up to the bench. The man is a psychologist and happened to have been there on another matter. The lieutenant talked at length to Hershel and reported back to the judge. The judge then asked Hershel to come forward."

"Life is hard enough," the judge said, "without adding layers of delusions."

"Alan, how do you know what was said in that court?"

"I called the clerk. She put me in touch with the lieutenant, Lt. Avram Brenner. Brenner said the judge was worried. He asked Hershel if it was his intention to do harm to himself. Hershel replied that he only wanted justice."

"If the courts don't punish you," the judge asked, "will you punish yourself? Are you likely to do harm to yourself?"

"The lieutenant told me that the question seemed to baffle Hershel. He put his hand to his chin and rubbed it as though the question had put him into deep contemplation. The judge pressed Hershel for an answer."

"When a system won't respond..." Hershel said, haltingly.

"Mr. Selden," said the judge, "let me warn you that you have taken yourself into a difficulty. If you leave me with the slightest impression that you might be a danger to yourself or others, then I am obliged to refer you to our mental health system for evaluation. Do you understand what I'm saying?"

"I'm not insane," Hershel said, "and if my understanding of responsibility is considered to be mental instability, then this whole society is insane. Do you understand me?"

"Only too well," said the judge. "Hershel Selden, I'm ordering Lt. Brenner to initiate a psychological review to determine whether or not you require treatment at this time for delusions which may or may not affect your future and the lives of those around you who are entitled to peaceful enjoyment within the State of Israel."

"Brenner told me that Hershel seemed stunned by what the judge had said. And as Hershel was about to leave, the judge told him to please go home and reflect on the many services he'd performed for his country, deeds which made the survival of Israel possible."

"How did Sarah and Hershel's two sons react to the fact that a psychological review had been ordered?"

"Nathan, Levi, and Sarah all tried to tell him that he'd piled too much guilt onto his own plate. Yes, the world of late had become complex, but in 1948 it was simple. Kill or be killed. Period."

Alan continued, "Nathan told me that Hershel said, 'So where does it stop?'"

"'You can't fix all that's happening; you were just one little soldier,' Nathan tried to tell him."

"'And so it goes, on and on,' Hershel replied, 'with every soldier everywhere. There's no stopping all that bloodshed unless I do what I can.'"

"At that point," Alan said, "the family realized the old man had crossed the line into insanity. He had undertaken a personal mission to cure the sins of this world."

"The next time you speak to your uncle, would you make sure to remember to give him my fondest regards?"

"That's a promise."

Chapter 7

Several days later, Anne received a voicemail message from Hershel saying he was staying at the Hyatt Regency in New Brunswick. He asked that she not call Alan. He wanted to talk to her alone. Anne was able to get to the hotel by mid-afternoon.

Hershel was sitting in the lobby when she arrived. Dressed in a blue suit and a white shirt without a tie, he sat staring at the long, wide, and elegantly carpeted stairway leading to the second floor's meeting rooms. Not wanting to startle him, she spoke his name softly. He stood and hugged her, thanking Anne for being there.

Looking around and seeing people in the lobby, he motioned for them to head up the stairs. On the second floor, to the right, a woman with a coffee cup was walking toward an open meeting room door. Hershel led Anne to the left, down a long empty corridor. He turned the handle on a large double door. It was unlocked. He ushered her slowly down the center isle of a softly lit paneled room that had been set up with hundreds of chairs facing a raised dais. Behind the dais was a screen some sixteen feet wide and fourteen feet high. Lighting came from rows of glass chandeliers with bulbs turned on at the dimmest setting.

Hershel and Anne walked up to the dais and took seats facing an audience of empty chairs.

"How have you been?" she asked.

"Alan told you about the referral for a psychiatric evaluation?"

"Yes."

"Going through that maze was an ordeal. But, it's been established. I'm not a crazy person to be medicated until my last breath."

"Where did Sarah and your sons, Nathan and Levi, stand during that difficulty?"

"They wanted me to be hospitalized and put on medication. The only condition of release would have been that I continue with the medication. It was a drug that made me forget. I begged Sarah not to go along with that program."

"Why was she so adamant?"

"In a word, I believe she considered what I was saying to be treasonous, treasonous against my family, my country, and my people."

"Did you see any truth in her position?"

"Yes, and I tried to put what had happened out of mind, but I could not. And when those ideas kept coming back, she told me that our differences had become too painful for her to deal with. She suggested that we separate until I come to my senses."

"Are you okay with that?"

"I love her as much today as when we first met, but the price she demands is too great."

Anne and Hershel sat in silence for a few moments. She imagined that Hershel was remembering highlights of his marriage and how he and Sarah struggled through the wars that followed in Israel. She was certain that he was remembering the births of their children and grandchildren.

Hershel broke the silence. "Bless Julia, the psychologist, and Avey, the lawyer. They saw me through the whole ordeal. Whatever happens, going forward, they will affirm I am not insane. You must meet them one day soon, Julia and Avey."

"You know, we never had a chance to finish our conversation," Anne said. "You told me that you were responsible for the deaths of Marion, Bill, Judith, Kevin, and Amy. We were in Alan's house, sitting by the window, and Sarah had asked you to stop talking about it. Remember?"

"Yes. I remember. I was going to tell you about what happened in the 1948 War, the War of Independence." Hershel leaned back in his chair, as if to make room for the cadre of people and the panoply of events that plagued his soul.

"My unit was on patrol outside of Jerusalem, on a road in an uninhabited area not far from where Marion's bus was blown up. It was dusk. Coming toward us was what looked like a family. An older man was pulling a cart that he'd tethered himself to by means of straps. Behind him, and holding onto the side of the cart, was a woman near the man's age. Walking to the rear was a young couple. Each was holding the hand of a child, young boys that I took to be about eight or nine years old.

"The leader of my unit ordered them to stop. The old man, speaking in Arabic, was saying something that we did not understand, but he was pointing up the road and to the right. I imagined he was saying they were returning to their home. By the way they were dressed, I took them to be farmers.

"We had previously ordered the Arabs from this area to leave their homes. And here they were, coming back. In the confusion, the young father stepped forward. The boy who had been holding his hand ran to his mother's side.

"The unit leader asked him to stop. It was unclear whether the young man heard or understood what was said. I started to walk toward the young man. He appeared to be unarmed, and I was holding a revolver."

"Why were you walking toward him?" asked Anne.

"I don't know. Just instinct. I wanted him to stop and get back with his family. He was crossing a line and he was totally unaware..." Hershel stopped talking and stared straight ahead into the middle of the huge room.

"Can you describe him?"

"Slightly taller than the man who was pulling the cart. Broad shouldered. Well muscled. And smiling. Some part of him was trying to engage us, man to man. The farm was only just over the hill, I imagined him thinking. They had come so far. The children would be glad to be in their own beds for a change. He was bringing all that information to us, and we would understand because we were all standing so very near the end of a sad, long march. And I imagined him at home, nodding and smiling to his wife and the two children. It would be the lore in his abode for generations to come that he had smiled them all back to the gates of their home and their farm."

Hershel then rose from his chair and looked at the big screen behind them. "The leader, Sergei Minkoff, that's what his name was. I was maybe twenty feet from the young man. Minkoff said 'Shoot the fucking bastard.' I looked at him, as though pleading for just a moment. No, just a few seconds to think. But he screamed at me, 'If you want freedom and dignity anywhere in this godforsaken world, then you'll shoot that fucking dog.'

"My gun went off as though it had a mind of its own. The bullet entered the young man's chest exactly where I imagined his heart would be. He crumpled to the ground.

"And it was as though my weapon had been tied to all the others. Minkoff began emptying rounds into the older man and the older woman, as he called upon the others in our unit to keep firing. 'The last thing we need are the haters in Israel, no matter what age,'" he screamed.

"My weapon might have fired again. I don't recall aiming it. I watched as the last light faded. The young mother and the two boys lay dead on the ground, bound together, clutching each other as their last acts on Earth. They were all dead. It was quiet."

Hershel seemed to watch them all for a short time on the screen behind us. "Then," he said, "we were ordered to move up the road. We took fire and fired back about a mile away. For the rest of the night, we hunkered down attempting to dislodge snipers from hilltops along the narrow road. Fighting in the weeks that followed was intense. I began to forget the killing of that young man who was moving toward me and how I participated in the murder of his family."

Anne didn't know what to say. The scene Hershel had painted suddenly became a part of her own interior landscape. She felt the weight of it upon her own soul.

She stood up and kissed Hershel on the cheek and held his hand as they sat next to one other. Both had been transported to that dark road outside of Jerusalem where lives had been so quickly extinguished.

"You began forgetting?" Anne asked.

"It was surprisingly easy. There was always talk about how Arabs had been murdering Jews for the past ten years. And there was some truth in that. Many of them hated our being allowed to come into their country. And there was always talk from one soldier or another about how they shot some Arab dogs or Arab pigs. Laughter became an affirmation. Laughter said that we would never allow what happened in Europe to happen again. Through it all, I remembered how close I came to being encircled by the young street Nazis. I might have been a day or two away from being struck with a pipe and left dead behind garbage cans in a Wurzburg street."

Some time went by. Hershel tightened his grip on Anne's hand and turned to her. "It was a bare-knuckled world back then. Survival demanded audaciousness. All of us knew what the cattle cars to Auschwitz looked like. None of us would ever consider climbing on board again. Never."

"So Julia and Avey understood why you shot that young Arab man?"

"Neither of them condoned what I did, but they apprehended the circumstances."

"At the same time, they honored your feelings of guilt."

"Exactly."

"They respected your connecting that crime to the deaths of Marion, Susan, Bill, and the children?"

"Yes. They said it was the epitome of taking responsibility."

Chapter 8

After they had dinner at the hotel, Hershel and Anne walked out into the chill spring evening up Albany Avenue and onto Easton. Easton Avenue had an eclectic mix of Asian, African, Middle East, and South American restaurants, along with an Irish bar, a used bookstore, bodegas, and places to buy telephones.

"I need to spend time right here," he said looking around at the ethnic array.

"Easton Avenue?" she said. "It's a draw for college kids who need to get away from dormitory food. What's the attraction for you?"

He laughed. "Maybe I have to distance myself from falafel and the constant admonitions that I should stop whining."

"The family?"

"And friends and neighbors. Word is out."

"That you're strange?"

"Worse. That I'm a traitor."

They walked past a coffee shop with an array of hookah pipes displayed in the window.

"I'm going stay at the hotel for a while and think things through."

"I'm sure Alan would be glad to have you. Why not stay with him?"

Hershel gave the question some thought. "Alan needs his hatred right now. That's all he has left. And he wouldn't understand what I'd be trying to do. If I were there, he'd feel like he was harboring a criminal."

"What is it you intend to accomplish while staying at the hotel?"

"Catch up with my life," he said. "From the beginning, it was formed by tragic circumstances over which I had no control. And I never had time to think things through for myself. Well, I'm taking that time now. And if I end up with a dumb question or two, would it be a bother if I could ask you about a few things as I go along?"

"Not at all," Anne replied.

For the next several months, Hershel made Rutgers University his home. Anne saw him on occasion at the library, taking notes with books piled around him. Realizing that there would be papers and essays on the internet that were not available to him with a guest library card, she took him to the office of the head librarian and said that Hershel was doing research for her. He should be accorded full library privileges for whatever he might need.

Early that summer, Alan called Anne to complain about his uncle. He'd been asking Alan to explain aspects of some legal cases that Hershel had been trying to understand.

"I'm sure it's just harmless curiosity," she said.

"But I have no stomach for it right now. I suggested he go home and stop rooting around in stuff like the Magna Carta and the Universal Declaration of Human Rights."

"What did he say to that?"

"He said he appreciated what I was telling him, but he wasn't quite ready to stop, go home, and sit on the porch. He needed a little more time."

"Alan, did he ever tell you what he did in the War of Independence that so bothers his conscience?"

"He did, and I said war is a bitch. Always was and always will be."

"What did he say to that?"

"I don't know. It sounded crazy. Something like all the children are as starbursts. Not really sure what the hell he meant. I just wanted to hang up the phone and not be listening to his foolish crap about the sanctity of life. I know all about that. Who knows more than I do about the sanctity of life?"

"So, how are you doing?" Anne asked.

"I'm trying to get on with things."

"And is that happening?"

"Yes. I just wish that Hershel would stop dragging his muddled junk past the memories of Marion and the children. It's," he paused, "disrespectful."

Anne told Alan she would talk to his uncle. Later that day, she found Hershel in the library and told him of her conversation with Alan.

"I understand. To him I must be both an imbecile and an embarrassment, as well as a betrayer of every Jew in the world."

"Well, I wouldn't go that far. I know he's concerned that you've isolated yourself and may be..."

"What? Out of touch with reality?" he said loudly. "Is that what you think too?"

Realizing that Hershel had started to shout, she took his arm and walked with him toward an exit.

"So, is that what you think too?" he repeated.

"No," Anne responded. "It's just a little sad. You come into this place," she waived her right hand upward to note that the library has long been a revered institution of learning. "You sit yourself down and fully expect that, what? You'll come up with a stunning revelation that no one before you has ever considered?"

Hershel stared at her and then looked down at the marble floor.

"It isn't that I agree with Alan," she continued. You're not a fool. I just want to warn you that these efforts of yours will more than likely be a torment," she hesitated before continuing, "at your age and under the sad circumstances that brought you here."

Tears began forming at the bottom of Hershel's eyes. They welled up and spilled over down his cheeks. He took a handkerchief out of his pocket and blotted his face. "The torment," he said, "is passing through this world like some dumb ox who was never expected to even begin figuring things out."

"You did the best you could."

"No. Something is wrong, terribly wrong. Shouldn't I be able to own up to my crimes?"

"I don't know what to say, Hershel. Maybe justice is not as perfect as we might want it to be."

"So, how does that help the next poor bastard from Honduras, Somalia, or India who's put in the same position as I was? How does he keep from being a murderer?"

Anne was impressed that Hershel's research had taken him to a recent coup against a democratic government, a totally failed state, and a country at war against its own people to accommodate mining and energy interests. "What can I do? How can I help?" she asked.

"I make Alan uncomfortable. Could you maybe make it possible for me to talk to teachers here about legal cases and about international law?"

"I'll speak to some law professors for you. If they're willing to answer your questions, I'll give you their names, telephone numbers, and areas of expertise. You'll have an initial list by tomorrow."

Hershel put his arms around Anne and hugged her softly. She felt the dampness on his cheeks and hugged him in return. In that brief moment, his breathing became deeper and surer. She had the sense that here was one of the loneliest souls in the world. An Israeli psychologist had struggled on his behalf to maintain the truth that he was not insane. And an Israeli lawyer had worked to keep Hershel from being considered a security risk. She felt obliged to be the third leg of the stool that promised him support for his final years. She would affirm the fact that he was not a fool.

Anne looked into his deep blue eyes. "Your nephew is not able, right now, to see you for the truly rational man that I think you are. He'll come around. Meanwhile, call me anytime you need help. And feel free to let me know what kind of ideas you're putting together. You good with that?"

"Thank you. I promise not to be a pest."

"What you're looking to do is laudable. Consider me an ally and a friend."

Chapter 9

In the months that passed, whenever Anne saw Hershel or Alan she encouraged the two of them to communicate with one another. They began to do so by letter. As if understanding the need for impartial assistance, they both sent her copies of their letters to each other.

Hershel began the correspondence by apologizing if his behavior was causing his nephew discomfort. Then, he stated, "My life has been mostly unexamined. Is it that way for most people?" he asked.

As she held her copy of the letter, Anne gave thought to his question. Narcissists spend huge amounts of time reflecting upon themselves. Hershel was clearly not one of that type. No, he was thinking about the roads that all of us were traveling, deeply examining issues involving war and peace.

How preciously rare was that undertaking, Anne thought, recalling how generations of Americans feared nuclear annihilation at any moment during the Cold War and mindlessly accepted the false assertions that there were no other options. And even knowledgeable historians refused to examine the propaganda being promulgated into government policy when they saw that speaking the truth could result in their being fired from employment or blackballed from creative projects. Only those who loudly trumpeted the falsehoods were assured continuous success in their endeavors.

So, here was Hershel, a man in his eighties, who for the first time in his life, was wrestling with the underpinnings that support the major assumptions of our time. His efforts would surely fail, she concluded. He had only two advantages, and they were both fairly weightless. First, he had the benefit of age and experience. Second, he was exploring world affairs for the first time and was thus unencumbered by a whole range of meaningless shibboleths and wrong-headed ideas. But death would likely take him, Anne concluded, sooner than he could see to the bottom of our tangled affairs and even begin to fashion remedies that might bring about betterment of any sort.

Alan wrote back, expressing his love and respect for his uncle. "If all men were as assiduous as you are for justice, this world would be a far different place." How nice, Anne thought, that Alan had been able to keep the fires of hatred that were consuming him from tarnishing his feelings of appreciation for Hershel.

Then came some very solid advice from Alan. "My own view of what you are doing is that you're unlikely to find any court to take your plea of guilty. In war, the ordinary rules of civilization don't seem to apply. In the end, you'll have to fashion your own response for the guilt that you've taken upon yourself."

Hershel's reply to that assertion was lengthy. He thanked Alan for the suggestion. It made sense. He asked whether setting up a foundation for peace might be helpful. His research, however, was that there might be too many of such endeavors. "Wouldn't creating another foundation for peace," he asked, "be like pissing in the wind?"

Anne laughed when she read Alan's reply. "Uncle. Save your precious bodily fluids. The winds of war blow at gale force. Unless you have some special idea in mind, creating another foundation would wind up just as you described. How are you doing with your search for a court that might take your plea?"

Hershel responded, saying that the search was turning out exactly as Alan had predicted. Israeli courts were out of the question. Courts in the United States would refuse to hear him because his crimes were committed elsewhere. The same was true for Courts in the European Union. And the International Criminal Court at The Hague, Hershel said, would not take a matter that involved acts that preceded its formation in 2002.

The last portion of the letter was a description of his efforts, with the help of a law professor from Rutgers, to have a criminal court in Spain hear his case. "It came to nothing," Hershel said. "The Spanish magistrate expressed regret. If they took my little case, he said, 'they would be inundated with a near endless number of battlefield offenses.'"

Anne was familiar with what Spain had accomplished. The legislature gave their courts universal jurisdiction to prosecute crimes wherever they occurred when it was clear that the country where the crime took place was unlikely to prosecute the guilty. Famously, a Spanish court initiated criminal cases against the Chilean dictator, General Augusto Pinochet, for tortures committed in Chile after 1973, when the United States engineered the overthrow of a democratically elected Chilean government and installed the General as dictator. A Spanish arrest warrant was served upon Pinochet while he was in England in 1998, and the highest court in England upheld the legality of the Spanish warrant the following year.

After that decision, a graduate student in one of Anne's classes, Tika Susila from Indonesia, expressed the hope that her parents had not died in vain. They'd been murdered, along with nearly a million others who were deemed leftists, by Suharto, a dictator put in power by the United States. Anne remembered Tika showing pictures to the class of her smiling parents and the pleasant village where she had been born and raised.

"I don't suppose," Alan wrote, "that you would want to enter your guilty plea in a Palestinian court?" Hershel replied that he did not wish to do so. He went on to try to explain his answer. It was a rambling explanation, Anne realized, because Hershel was grappling with the arbitrariness surrounding how people are or are not recognized in the existing world order.

It wasn't that he disrespected their courts, but "it's not even a country, Alan. They are considered just observers to the United Nations." Hershel went on, "Observers in a world that has no rational way to make up its mind about these kind of things. I'm finding that there are groups of people who don't even have the status of observers. They've been trapped in countries for a century after borders had been drawn by colonial powers purposely to make cohesive national efforts impossible. And aboriginal people can be treated as though they never existed at all. What should they be called, optionally observable humans? I cannot believe this planet is as uncivilized as it is, and I've only just begun to see things for what they really are. Palestine," he told his nephew, "is little likely to become a member of the United Nations. That being the case, its courts have a status similar to tribal councils."

Alan replied in writing, "You've done all you can. It's time to go home."

It was mid-summer when Anne called Hershel and invited him to her home for dinner. She lived in a modest one family house in nearby Franklin Township. He came to door with a small basket of fresh fruit, wearing open leather shoes, khaki pants, and a light blue pullover shirt. She'd never seen him dressed so casually. In that outfit, with his well-tanned body and muscular build, she mused that he had easily erased the ten or twelve year difference in their ages.

"Look at you," she said laughing. "I thought you only owned suits, white shirts, and monochromatic ties."

"You know I help coach the soccer team at your school."

"I had no idea."

"Well, I do, and when I kept showing up at practice in my suits, they threatened to go on strike. They left me no choice."

As the two of them settled in the back yard with cold drinks, Anne brought up Alan's last letter, the one that said it was time for Hershel to end his efforts.

"I'm supposed to go home now. You read it too?"

"You did try, Hershel, harder than anyone could ever imagine. And I will never forget you."

He said nothing for a long time and looked around the back yard with its long lawn and scattered rose bushes around the edges. Anne broke the silence. "I don't know if it's any consolation, but I've begun telling my students about you."

"What's their reaction?" he asked. "An old fool who can't figure out what side he's on? That's what I imagine."

"Not exactly," she told him. "The Jewish kids tend to think that you did what you had to do. My Arab students want me to thank you for expressing a difficult point of view."

"And the others?" he asked.

"Could not imagine ever being ordered to kill innocent people."

"And when called upon to go to war someplace for the stupidest of reasons, against people who meant them no harm," he said, "they'll all just plunge right in and end up killing innocent people. Isn't that about correct?"

"Wars are everywhere. It's always been so, Hershel, and it looks as though it will always be the case. You've set your sights too high if you think you can do anything to stop the process."

"So Amy and Kevin died for nothing? That's what you're saying?"

"I wish I could disagree, but I can't. I just teach history. I don't make it. I don't influence it. For me, history rolls on of its own accord. Over time, there are small gains. Do you know what my doctoral thesis was on? Did I ever tell you?"

"No, you never did."

"My thesis was about how one man in the eighteen hundreds, King Leopold of Belgium, was able to personally own and enslave the very heart of Africa, the Congo. That's not going to happen again. We've made some progress, wouldn't you say?"

"Hitler and the Holocaust is progress?" Hershel replied sharply. "And just how many Armenians thinking back to the slaughter in Turkey would agree with you? Pol Pot in Cambodia was what, chairman of a debating society? And souls of Tutsis who were murdered by Hutus in Rwanda might say that you're deluded."

"As I said before, I just teach history. I don't make it." She reached across the table and put her hand on his. "And as much as I respect you, Hershel, please understand that you don't make it either."

Hershel turned his hand upward so that the two of them were holding hands as he continued looking out at the backyard. "I'll be doing some traveling in Europe for a time," he said.

"What will you be doing?"

"I'll be forum shopping. That's the phrase the lawyers use."

Anne laughed. "It's not like you to give up, is it?"

"Correct. But I have another favor to ask. I miss working with soil and planting seeds to grow fruits and vegetables." He gripped her hand just a little bit tighter. “Would you consider allowing me to do that in your yard? You may keep everything that grows,” he said, turning to her, “or we might share it all together.”

“Yes,” she responded, with a broad smile, imagining them both working in the garden, weeding and pruning and stopping for an occasional kiss, “if that’s what you would like.”

Chapter 10

Perhaps they were all correct, and he was a fool, Hershel thought, as the airliner reached its cruising altitude on the way to Europe. Anne had said it several days before when he had dinner at her home. Hadn't he done his best? Alan said the same thing. And here he was on his way to the courts in Spain, France, and the Netherlands to make one last pitch, personally. It was a practice he'd undertaken in business. Refusals by potential buyers were often mistakes in communication. Sometimes by merely showing up, a sale could be made. Showing up was a display of pride in ones work and an indication that Selden's company would stand behind its products.

The discussion with Assistant Prosecutor, Juan Moret, in Madrid was brief. Moret expressed his regret that Spain was limiting its use of universal criminal jurisdiction. "I think we're getting out of the business," he said with a downcast look. "The dream of one generation of politicians too quickly becomes the bane of the next."

In Strasbourg, France, a clerk at the European Court of Human Rights told Hershel that the man with whom he had an appointment was unavailable. He then scolded Hershel for not knowing that his offense had to have occurred in Europe. "And did you not take the time to discover," the clerk asked icily, "that we only entertain cases on appeal from the highest courts in Europe?"

The International Criminal Court at The Hague, in the Netherlands, is located in a series of white buildings, some twenty stories high. Two of them stand at angles to one another with an entrance in between, looking much like pages in an open book. Hershel appreciated that imaginative touch as he approached the doors.

He went to the front desk in the lobby, told a young man behind the counter of his appointment with a Ms. Zender. Within moments, a comely woman in her forties, wearing a dark suit approached him.

"I am Assistant Prosecutor Marianne Zender. You are Hershel Selden?" The two shook hands. "Is this your first visit to the Netherlands?" she asked. Hershel understood her purpose in asking the question. She had deviated from the usual procedures when she penned a short note to the bottom of an official letter rejecting his application. It said, "If your travels take you to the Netherlands, please call. I would like to know more about what you call instigative causers." Now, this person unknown to her, a confessed murderer, had actually come to see her. She felt it necessary to elicit a response from which she could determine something about his state of mind. Was he, perhaps, unbalanced, a danger to others? Should he be allowed into the workspaces of ICC personnel?

"This is my first visit, and it's obvious. I wasted my time living elsewhere."

"You must call me Marianne. May I call you Hershel?"

They took an elevator to the fifth floor and walked down a corridor with offices on both sides of the hallway. All were filled with people pouring over documents, chatting, and looking at computer screens. Marianne said, "You know, I found your application fascinating."

"So, you intend to give me the courtesy of a final rejection in person?"

"More or less." They both laughed.

They went into her office, a comfortable workspace with a steel desk, several chairs, and a couch piled up with papers and transcripts. A secretary brought coffees for them.

Sitting across the desk from Hershel, Marianne asked, "Would you mind if I record this conversation?"

"Not at all," Hershel responded. "Just one condition, that you send it around this place."

"I'll do my best," she said, pressing the record button on a device that sat on the desk between them.

"Very few people make the argument that you do about getting to the root causes of war and turmoil," Marianne said.

"That's because the people you listen to are lawyers. Didn't your mother give you proper warnings about lawyers?"

"She's one herself."

"God help you."

"Let's be clear," Marianne said. "This tribunal will only take jurisdiction concerning actual war crimes and only those committed after 2002 when the Court was created. And that doesn't sit well with you?"

"Correct."

"Why?"

"Because you're not coming anywhere near stopping the violence. If you continue with such a narrow focus, you'll have to build ten of these facilities in every major city in the world, just to keep up with rising tides of murder and mayhem in the world."

The two of them sat quietly, sipping coffee. "You focus on the crimes committed by an actor at the very endpoint," he continued, "and you give those people who were the instigators a free pass and all the encouragement they need to continue their deadly operations."

"Give me an example," Marianne said, looking at the recording machine.

"Okay," he said, "a couple of instigators, let's say people in leadership positions in one of the dominant countries of the world, undermine a functioning democracy and install a mentally unstable dictator. The instigators follow that up by giving him enormous amounts of weaponry, which he uses against his own people and against neighboring countries."

"And we prosecute the war crimes which result from that scenario," Marianne responded.

"But one active instigator," Hershel responded, "can outpace you by bringing mayhem to scores of places, each one then experiencing waves of violence that will take hundreds of thousands of lives for the next several generations."

Hershel got up from his chair and went to the door. Opening it, he let in the sounds of workplace conversations and noises from computers and printers. "In the end, with all that," he said, referring to the sounds coming from busy workplaces, "you take pride when you catch up with a colonel from Guatemala or a major in Chile. You prosecute them when they're as old as I am, hoping they make it to the end so that you can claim a victory."

"You're not being very charitable," Zender said.

"No," Hershel responded, closing the door slowly and leaning against it until the latch sounded with a small click, "because from the time some instigators did their deeds until the time you prosecuted a few aging colonels and majors, a dozen instigators will have created a myriad of hells on Earth. The instigators—and there are so many of them—easily outpace you. You won't ever confront them. Justice is rarely, if ever, served."

Walking toward his chair, Hershel added, "At the very least, just start prosecuting the instigators who did their dirty work after the year 2002."

Hershel sat down. "And what I'm offering," he said, "is a chance to begin prosecuting them. Just take jurisdiction, as you say, of my case."

"It occurred before 2002."

"But it resulted in murders in 2007, and, in any event, I waive that defense."

"Your killing an Arab family cannot be tied causally to a suicide bomber in Israel who took the lives of your family members so many years later."

"I'm totally baffled," Hershel responded. "How did the law decide to focus so narrowly? My war crime contributed to a wellspring of fury that obviously fueled the actions of Rami Abu Mussel in April of 2007."

"You know, Hershel, I'm not disagreeing with you. But we had to start somewhere."

"Fine," he said, "but don't end up where you started if where you started won't lead to the goal of justice for all."

Marianne led her guest out of the building. She thanked him at the entranceway for stopping by. "Some of my colleagues agree with you. I'll be talking to them about our conversation. Maybe, hopefully, I'll get back to you."

"Better work fast," he smiled, "I can't remember what I had for breakfast."

"Take this," she said, handing Hershel a piece of paper with the name Klaus Steiner and a telephone number written on it. "He's in Karlsruhe. I don't hold out any hope for what you're trying to do, but you should at least talk to Steiner. I told him you'd be calling."

Klaus Steiner, a lawyer in Karlsruhe, Germany had the look of someone who'd been seriously imposed upon. "And just how do you know Marianne Zender?" he asked.

"After I described my case to her," Hershel said smiling, "she said it was unlikely to be successful. Then she gave me your name."

Steiner, a well-dressed man in his sixties started to reach for the phone and then stopped himself. After a moment of thought, he began asking Hershel about the details of his matter. In a few hours, that information had been dictated in the form of affidavits to a secretary and returned for Hershel's signature.

"This world of ours," the lawyer said as Hershel was leaving, "defies the kind of reasoning that you bring to it."

"I wasted your time."

After Hershel, in the bar at the hotel in New Brunswick, described his trip to Anne, she said, "You didn't waste anyone's time."

"Including yours?"

"Least of all mine." She reached across the table in the bar and held his hand.

"Have you given any thought to my job application?" he asked, laughing softly.

"I'm not sure..."

"Your home needs a full time gardener," he interrupted.

Anne sat back in her chair and considered what he was saying. Hershel waited as several emotions played across her face.

"As long as you stay in touch with Sarah," Anne said, "and agree to reunite with her if and when she wishes you to do so."

"There's little likelihood of that," he said, "because I'll never change my thinking about being responsible for the deaths of Marion and the children. And I will never agree to be silent about it."

"Of course," she said.

The two of them slowly leaned forward over the small table. They kissed gently. Their lips barely touched, but it was in that small contact that they shared an understanding. Neither of them would be alone, and both would be free to love each other and to explore bold thinking about a better future.

Chapter 11

A year had passed since Hershel's meeting with Klaus Steiner in Karlsruhe, Germany. During that time, the lawyer had stayed in touch with him, occasionally asking for additional information and copies of documents. He called one morning and spoke to Anne.

"Any news to report?" she asked.

"Possibly. But I need Hershel to come to my office. Do you think he might be up to that?"

Anne laughed. "Are you kidding? That man dug and planted a garden that takes up most of my back yard. He coaches soccer, keeps up with his business, and he's in the library twenty-five hours every week, catching up with the damn sad history of this world. Does that answer your question?"

"My God, does the idea of retirement ever come up?"

"Never enters his mind."

"What's his secret?"

Anne thought a moment. "He's open to discovery in a way that few people experience. Learning is an elixir for him."

"Well, tell him to get to my office. He'll be interested in learning about the stir that his case is making."

"Can I give him some idea of what it's about?"

"Sure. Hershel is demanding that the legal system live up to the goals it set for itself."

"Any likelihood of that happening?"

"Not a chance," said Steiner, "but he should know, first-hand, what people are saying about him."

Hershel made the necessary arrangements and within days was in Steiner's office for an early morning conference.

"When you walked in here," the attorney said, smiling, "I should have closed my door and pretended I was sleeping. Then, some young fool in this practice would have been saddled with your case."

Hershel smiled back as the two of them walked toward Steiner's wide, dark, and richly ornamented wooden desk. The lawyer's suit had been crafted exactly to fit his thin, short frame. Sitting required that he unbutton his jacket. Black pearl cufflinks appended to a white embroidered shirt came together in that process. "You see, Hershel, that was a year ago, almost to the day. I was ready to retire. My wife was expecting me to help her make plans to travel. I was ready, and then you descended upon the legal practice of Steiner, Fuchs, and Burhoff."

"I don't understand," Hershel said, smiling. "Mine is the easiest case of all. Killing is killing. What am I missing?"

"What you're missing is that the German legal system is one of the most sensitive in the world. It doesn't just deal with the surface layers of cases that come before it. Its tendency is to get to the bottom, to the root causes of things."

"Fine words," Hershel said, "but it's hard for me...My memories loom large."

"I understand."

"So where was this great system when it was needed most?" Hershel asked.

"Eclipsed by the Nazis." Neither men spoke. "But before you close that case in your mind," Steiner said, "understand that Hitler was paid for and supported, in large part, by major economic figures and corporations of the day, on *both* sides of the Atlantic," he added with emphasis. "And they wanted him because he opposed the communists who threatened to end the primacy of property. Once in office, Hitler picked perverse people to help him lead. Together, they unleashed the most brutal aspects of human nature. My colleagues in the law and on the bench, scholarly and reserved, could not stop such an ugly and powerful onslaught."

"It's that brutal part that sticks in my mind."

"Please consider, at least for now," said Steiner, "that the beast resides throughout the world and even in those two places you've chosen to reside."

Steiner paused and then continued, "We don't have time for that discussion. Getting back to the German legal system. It was eclipsed by the Nazis, but the wellsprings from whence it came are intact."

"And they are?"

"Number one, a long line of philosophers who sought both truth and justice. Number two, all of our decisions were made by judges, not juries. And the third item is a new Constitution that was put into effect after the Second World War."

"Interesting."

"Yes. You can study all that later. Anne told me how assiduous a researcher you are. I only brought the subject of German legal competence up so that you might have confidence to face what I've agreed to put you through later this morning."

"What is it you're having me go through?"

"A questioning at the office of the Prosecutor. You see, your offer to admit guilt has touched off a far-ranging conversation between the Offices of the Prosecutor, the Criminal Court judges, and our Constitutional Court judges. You were wrong earlier. Killing is not just killing. They will want to know all about you, and all about the circumstances that brought about the offense.

Hershel, Under German criminal jurisprudence, nothing is off the table."

"And the purpose?"

"To find where lies true responsibility."

"That's what the meeting with the Prosecutor is about later this morning?"

"Exactly. And with my permission, you will be placed under oath. The Prosecutor will ask any questions of you that he wishes. I want you to go slowly through this process. Try to understand each and every question. Give thought to the answers, and respond as honestly as you possibly can."

Steiner laughed, "Your case is a puzzle. You are an enigma. Opinions about you differ widely. I, myself, believe that you are something like a modern Christ figure, a killer come to say don't do what I did."

Hershel laughed. "I want another lawyer."

"Too late for that now. Our appointment is 10:30."

A taxi took them to the offices of the Attorney General of Germany. The building, unlike most of Karlsruhe, was modern in style. It reminded Hershel of the straight clear lines of the International Criminal Court at The Hague.

"We have an appointment with Mr. Egon," Steiner said to the receptionist. Hershel glanced up at the wall behind the desk and saw a picture of Frederick Egon, under which were the words, Attorney General of Germany.

Hershel turned to Klaus. "You didn't tell me..."

"I did not want you to be nervous. It's just a conversation you'll be having."

They were led into a library by a secretary and sat at a long conference table. "Why would the Attorney General, himself, be calling me in here for a conversation?"

"Your case," said Steiner, "has put him into a unique position. You have waived rights that other defendants never waive, including the fact that the crime occurred before the law that allows for war crime prosecutions. You have waived your right to contend that the State of Israel and only Israel must prosecute you. Biggest of all, you have waived your right to say that your crime in Israel in 1948 had nothing causally to do with the deaths of your family in a suicide bombing outside of Jerusalem on April 10th of 2007."

"Yes. Yes, I have."

"Well, Mr. Egon is entitled to know, for himself, whether you are, the way Americans say it, a nutcase or not."

"But I still don't understand why it has to be Egon, himself, to talk to me?"

"Because," Steiner said, "this matter of yours has enormous implications."

"Implications. Yes," said the Attorney General, as he entered the room, shook hands with Klaus and extended his hand to Hershel. Egon was tall and angular. His face reflected kindness, authority, and professionalism. "Your application to enter a guilty plea here has implications beyond anything I could have imagined. Let me just say that a criminal court is assessing the case. That you know. But, because your application is so unusual, the criminal court judges have made a request of the Constitutional Court for assistance."

Steiner laughed, "Freddie, at this rate I will never fucking retire."

"It gets worse," Egon said. "The judges of both courts have determined that they will apprise the Bundestag and the Bundesrat of their rulings. Not that the federal legislature will necessarily weigh in, but the judges believe that the lawmakers could well be affected by decisions they may be making."

"Shit," said Klaus. "The press will jump all over these proceedings. We'll be ground into pulp and then be thrown out onto the internet."

"Don't listen to him. Your lawyer is an old ham. He'll be lavishing the attention."

"So," the Attorney General said, "these are among the reasons you are here today. I'm going to ask you a number of questions. The purpose is for me to be satisfied with the underpinnings of the case. I can call a halt to going any further. Do you understand that?"

Hershel nodded that he did. "Something about discretion that you have," he said.

"It's a limited discretion. I must be certain, however, before having this case go on, that you are..."

"Of sound mind," Hershel said.

"Correct, and did your lawyer also say that I may ask you any questions that I wished? You are to answer them with candor and without evasion of any sort?"

"Yes, he said that."

"Let me add that every word the two of us say in this room is to be taken down by a stenographer so that a permanent record is created here. Do you agree with that being done?"

"Yes."

"Your lawyer, the eminent Klaus Steiner, has agreed not to object to any of my questions. Do you understand that, as well?"

Hershel looked over to Klaus. Steiner nodded his approval. "It's the least I can do for a Prosecutor who may just be putting his life's work and sterling reputation on the line for a wacko who should, at this very moment, be sitting in a café in Tel Aviv, overlooking the Mediterranean, watching some of the most beautiful women in the world pass by."

"You know, I tried to fire him this morning," Hershel said.

Egon laughed as he picked up the phone on the library table and asked for the stenographer to come in. Hershel began to experience a shortness of breath and the onset of anxiety.

Steiner seemed to read his mind. "Just take your time. Answer the questions as honestly as you can. You'll be fine, Hershel Selden. I believe in you."

Chapter 12

Egon began the deposition by noting, for the record, the date, November 4, 2009, the place, and the people in the room. The purpose of the questioning, he said was "to ascertain more about the character and motivation of the defendant, Hershel Selden.

"Mr. Selden, your attorney has, on your behalf, filed a voluminous affidavit that sets forth the details of your application to the Court. Has he shared with you why your application is quite unusual?"

"Yes. He has. Mr. Steiner told me that I have waived every possible defense to the crime."

"So, in most circles, people who put themselves at risk, as you are doing, when to do so is unnecessary, might be called self destructive and possibly insane. Mr. Selden, do you fall into that category?"

"God no," Hershel replied. "It's the world that's insane, and absurd as well," he added quickly.

"Beside yourself, are there others who see things as you do?"

"Yes, of course. What I'm saying is obvious. What's being portrayed as reality is, in fact, a dangerous delusion."

"What makes you say that the world is insane and absurd?"

"It refuses to learn from experience."

"What do you mean by that?"

"Look, the use of new weaponry made the First World War more deadly than any other war in all of recorded history. So, when it was over, there should have been a world body created to stop the lunacy that might, in the future, lead to more wars. That didn't happen. It was less than fifteen years later that absolutely nightmarish behavior started coming out of Germany. And there was no world body to stop it."

"And you mean by nightmarish behavior?"

"The claim that the Arian Race was superior. The pronouncement that Jews were evil and responsible for all that was wrong in the world. Those two dangerous lies could be trumpeted endlessly because there was no world body to uphold truth."

"Mr. Selden, isn't the United Nations the world body that you're calling for?"

"No. It cannot correct untruths, and it cannot come anywhere near keeping the peace."

"Why do you say that?"

"It's not just me taking that position, Mr. Egon. Every thoughtful historian I've read over the last several years agrees. That body is inadequate."

"Mr. Selden, why are you so adamant concerning this point?"

Hershel took a deep breath and quietly said, "That failing made me a killer, and my killing led to the murder of my family in retaliation."

"Would you kindly be more explicit?"

"I was ordered to execute a young Arab man who was standing, unarmed, some twenty feet from me, and I did as I was ordered."

"Do you defend that action as being appropriate?"

"No. Murder is never appropriate, but I felt it was required of me."

"Why do you say that?"

"Because justice was unattainable. Your United Nations had created two states within Palestine. The American president recognized Israel within minutes of our declaration of statehood. That all sounded so wonderful. But it was just foolishness. Words. Empty words. A properly functioning United Nations would have rushed in troops to keep the peace. Sending in troops was beyond the capacity of the United Nations because it had no authority or resources to do so. It was all just words. Empty words."

There was silence in the room. Hershel continued, "The Jews deserved better. The Arabs deserved better. We were left with the obligation to fight it out. Freedom to be at each other's throats. Barbarity covered over with the cloak of international order. It was insane and absurd. The murders went on in Israel and throughout the world. They continue to this day."

"Mr. Selden, you know that we in Karlsruhe and our colleagues on the International Criminal Court do our utmost to bring people to justice for war crimes and crimes against humanity. We prosecute them."

"No, on rare occasions you prosecute a head of government or a military leader. That allows you to keep up an illusion that you're stopping the destruction. In reality, you have tried maybe a handful out of many thousands of people throughout the world who deserve to be prosecuted." Selden looked at Egon, trying to measure his next words, fearing what their impact on this man, the Attorney General, might be. "It's a paltry effort, and I didn't come all this way and put myself in jeopardy to hear you say that you're doing it well and that all is well."

Steiner whistled briefly and nodded at Egon. "Wish I had said that."

Egon, turning to Hershel said, "I thank you for your advice. It's admirable that you wish to stop warfare. Doubtful, however, that either you or I or Mr. Steiner or scores of Egons and Steiners who will follow us will ever stop warfare. So, perhaps we should content ourselves just to go on with your case."

"Of course. I aimed for the young man's heart, wishing his death would be swift. Killing him was the only possible way for me to live with any dignity and freedom 'in this godforsaken world,' as my commanding officer had put it. Then I continued shooting. I may have——I'm not sure——put bullets in the wife and the children. The gun emptied itself."

"Godforsaken world?" asked Egon.

"What else would you call it?" Hershel shot back. "My family was gassed to death by the Nazis. Arab nations threatened to throw me into the sea. And there was no international body to stop them. Only street gang justice. The world has progressed little beyond street gang justice."

"Yes, I'm familiar with your Wurzburg experiences."

"The night I murdered that young Arab man, I had a dream."

"I'm not sure we're interested in dreams," Egon said.

Steiner replied, "I suggest you listen to this one." He nodded for Hershel to continue.

"I dreamed that I was a small wooden puppet on strings held far above me by dark, brooding figures. My mother and father were trying to cut the strings. With them was Fritz Wiedemann. The three of them were trying to cut the strings. But they were pushed aside by the shadowy figures above, and the strings became tighter."

"And this dream is supposed to mean what?" asked Egon.

"The dream says it all," said Steiner. "The boy's parents and people like Wiedemann, who tried to warn the world about Hitler, were pushed aside. After that, Hershel became a puppet in all the horrors that followed. Carl Jung would say that Hershel's dream came from the collective unconscious. Who was not a mere puppet in the destruction that followed? Are we not all puppets in the destruction that continues to this very day?"

Egon turned to Hershel. "Your lawyer, who has suddenly become a Jungian psychiatrist, says there is great meaning in your dream. Do you agree?"

Hershel shook his head as if he did not know. "You'll have to say yes or no for the record," the Prosecutor said.

"I don't know, except to say that my mother and father spoke often of Fritz Wiedemann who tried so mightily to stand against Hitler's rise. And they read the *Munich Post*, expecting that Hitler's lies would be exposed and that he would be stopped. Instead, Wiedeman and the *Post* were stopped and then forgotten. And all those who fed, helped, and propped up the Nazis were never called to account. I don't know about psychiatry, but shouldn't those kinds of things be a part of what you and the Court look at?"

"And exactly what in particular are you saying that we should be looking at?" asked Egon. "No," Egon said, addressing the stenographer. "Strike that question from the record. It's not for this man to be setting our agenda. I don't know what I was thinking."

"Frederick, for what it's worth, please allow him to answer," said Steiner. "You may find out that he's fully delusional. If so, you can then use your discretion to ask the Court to dismiss his application."

"Alright," said Egon with distain, "answer the question. What are you, Hershel Selden, saying that our most venerable Court, sitting in Karlsruhe, Germany should be doing that it's not already doing?"

"There ought to be," Hershel said, "some way for the Court to help people who are trying to keep peace and order in the face of big lies and distortions. At the same time, your Court needs to be punishing not just war criminals, but the instigators who create disorders out of which wars and war crimes arise."

"Now, these so-called instigators..." Egon began.

"I'm just an old man, not an expert, but I've come up with scores of them."

"Feel free," said the Attorney General.

"The case I most think about is the assassination of young Patrice Lumumba. Thin, eloquent, scholarly, he was the first democratically elected prime minister of the Congo in 1961. That was the last chance for peace in the Congo. The Belgians and the Americans had him murdered. Almost fifty years later..." Hershel stopped speaking and stared vacantly in the direction of the stenographer.

"Mr. Selden," said Egon.

"Is it fifty years now? The whole of central Africa is still on fire. I don't know, have the deaths and dislocations reached ten million people? Twenty million? You have to tell me."

There was silence at the table. Hershel continued. "Is there any promise for peace since Patrice was murdered? You may be prosecuting people who are distantly connected to his murder. That monstrous crime against humanity occurred fifty years ago, but the instigators, Americans and Belgians, were allowed to cover themselves with honor, while you looked the other way."

"Well, it's up to you, Frederick," said Steiner. "Weigh in. Is this man a nutcase or does he make sense?"

"I think that will be all for today," Egon said.

Chapter 13

"Don't tell me you hired another gardener," Hershel said when Anne answered his call from Kalsruhe.

"I'm only interviewing," she responded, laughing.

"I'll be leaving on United flight #8249 tomorrow morning at 10:05."

"Can't wait. I'll pick you up. I miss you."

"Me too," he said.

The next day, Anne stood at the bottom of the escalator in the baggage claim area at Newark Airport. Hershel noticed the concerned look on her face. That look turned into a broad smile when they saw each other and hugged.

"You thought they would lock me up and throw the key away."

"That's what you had hoped for," she said laughing. "Everything's backwards with us, isn't it?"

"I don't know how this will turn out, but I've done all that I can. It's up to them now."

"How were things left?"

"At present, the case is on some kind of hold while the Justices are communicating with one another. Something about getting an opinion from what Steiner said was the Constitutional Court. A lot of what's going on is beyond my knowing at this time.

"Oh, one thing is interesting. You're looking at the defendant in docket number E4178P12, but don't be surprised if they start referring to it as The Puppet's Case. They use designations like that in an effort to maintain the anonymity of litigants."

"Interesting," said Anne. "Tell me how they came to be thinking of that name for your case."

Standing a dozen feet behind Hershel and Anne was a comely woman in her sixties with graying hair holding an oversized pocketbook. The outside of her pocketbook was decorated with a large silver flower that was a directional microphone. Through earphones she listened to the conversation between Hershel and Anne.

Then came an interruption by a male voice. "Good feed, Silver. Keep the distance. Carousel 9? On the way to you. Good. Overseer 9 in place."

"Well, I'm intrigued," Anne said, laughing. "Hitler was famous for removing identities and replacing them with numbers? Now the Germans are hiding your ordinary identity and replacing it with a fascinating *nom de guerre* that might just make you into a movie idol."

"Everything is backwards, isn't it?" he responded.

They walked toward the baggage claim area, holding hands. A man with a cell phone camera snapped several pictures of them without aiming as Hershel and Anne walked toward the carousels. Silver followed, making sure no one got between her and the targets.

"By the way," Hershel said, "consider yourself lucky. While I was in the neighborhood, I looked up my old girlfriend, Solveg."

"When you say old, you do mean old."

"Your luck. Solveg's mother answered the door and told me that she wouldn't let her daughter come out and play. She, the mother, didn't like me back then and she can't stand me now. That was the end of what could have been a beautiful story."

They laughed and held one another closely as they approached an electronic board that directed them to Carousel 9.

The woman with the silver pocketbook stood behind them, listening. She heard a command directive, "Overseer up. Silver to Exit Door 3." Silver turned and walked to the Exit Door 3. A 14 inch microphone and camera installed above Carousel 9 honed in on Hershel and Anne.

"I think I know why the Attorney General of Germany, himself, is involved with your case."

"Yes, that was a surprise."

"I believe," Anne said, "he's involved because there's been pressure to give up undertaking universal criminal jurisdiction cases in Germany."

"Pressure from where?"

"Not sure. Could be groups that want to limit government or just want to take Germany out of that difficult role. You know, leave all of that business up to the International Criminal Court."

"How did you come upon this information?"

"Been looking at the German newspapers," she replied.

"What has all that to do with Egon being so involved with my case?"

"Well, the opposition, as a fallback position, wants to limit Germany's taking universal criminal jurisdiction only to cases involving German citizens anywhere in the world."

"So, that leaves me out."

"Not so, Hershel. Their Constitution grants German citizenship to all people who were forced out of Germany during the Nazi era. All you have to do is apply."

"You can't mean they would allow me, a confessed war criminal, to become a citizen just by applying."

"I don't know for sure, but that's where the designation of Puppet may become important."

"Sorry, you lost me."

"Egon and others within the German leadership want to uphold universal criminal jurisdiction, but there's opposition. Along comes Hershel's case. You are the epitome of that kind of jurisdiction. You, like a puppet, were made to kill people. Maybe some of the judges are thinking that yours is a universal problem. If it could happen to you, then it could happen to any of us. So, you might be thought of as the poster boy for the very concept of universal criminal jurisdiction."

"Maybe I have jet lag. Can you make that clearer?"

"Okay. Egan resists those who would shut down universal criminal jurisdiction by putting an emphasis on your case. Why? Your case, unless I'm wrong, says it all. Your case is the most powerful argument possible in favor of the need to keep plugging way at universal criminal jurisdiction."

The two of them were quiet for a moment. Anne continued. "Free will is an illusion if, in fact, we're all being manipulated, like puppets. So, Egon may be trying to find a way to give us all back our human dignity."

"Human dignity, a wonderful concept. How might that be entering into his thinking?"

"I'm just guessing, but when I looked at the German Constitution to find out about your status as a citizen, I noticed the opening paragraphs. Human dignity is the very first right granted to all German citizens, the inviolable right to human dignity."

"And they mean it?"

"I think so, yes. Your case may become very significant. Puppetry and human dignity are mutually exclusive."

Hershel retrieved his suitcase from the conveyor. When he joined Anne, she said, "And human dignity, by the way, is the first principle in the Universal Declaration of Human Rights."

"But that Declaration," said Hershel, "I came across it in my reading. It's just an expression of opinion from the General Assembly. All just words that were never approved by the Security Council. So, the Declaration doesn't ever begin to be enforceable anywhere."

"Correct, but if Egon has his way," Anne responded, "he would make it enforceable, using the Courts of Germany as they undertake universal criminal jurisdiction. As I said, your case can conceivably become very significant. Are you ready for that to happen, Mr. Puppetman?"

Hershel, rolling a suitcase toward the woman standing at Exit Door 3, who was designated as Silver, said, "Go figure. This dung heap of murder and oppression..."

"That's going on everywhere," Anne interrupted.

"May end," Hershel continued, "with a stroke of luck combined with mercy from, of all places, the home of the very Satan who drove me to Palestine and my experience as a war criminal."

"All backwards," Anne smiled. "I'm just happy that Solveg's mother answered the door, not Solveg. By this time, I'd be receiving a Dear Anne letter."

Chapter 14

Wilfred Schoft ate his breakfast mechanically that morning. He gently cracked the tops off of two soft-boiled eggs as they sat up in tiny porcelain cups with bold drawings of chickens. The cups with chickens were his wife's, Ingrid's, idea. Born and raised on a farm in a rural area southwest of Dresden, she wanted their children to remember where food comes from.

As Wilfred, lost in thought about his latest assignment at the Court, buttered his toast, he heard Ingrid say, "Earth to Wilfred. Earth to Wilfred. Do you read me? Come in, Wilfred."

He smiled over the top of his wire rimmed glasses. His long, thin face transformed in an instant from somber to sorry and then to amusement. Running a hand quickly through long dark hair, he asked, "Was I that far from base? Really?"

"You had rounded Mars and were heading out to Neptune."

"I'm sorry," he said and laughed. "Eric and John, do you ever get so involved in something you're thinking about that Mom has to give you a shout to get you back to Earth?"

"Nooo," they both said, smiling at their father.

"Alright, off to school," she said, "the two of you. Everything is in your backpacks. Love you both." The boys ran toward the vestibule where Ingrid had placed their backpacks, the green one for Eric and the blue one for John. Their school was a few blocks from home in a middle class neighborhood of Karlsruhe. Later that morning, Ingrid would take a bus to a nearby hospital, where she was a nurse. Wilfred would drive to his work at the Court.

"Is something troubling you?" she asked, tilting her head quickly to the left and hefting her long blond hair back over her shoulders as she cleared dishes from the table and headed toward the sink.

"This case," he said. "It's been kicking around for over a year now."

"Why so long?" she asked.

"My Presiding Judge..."

"Fritz Leber," she interrupted. "Have you told him that I would leave you in a minute for him?"

"What a waste of energy. He's just an older version of me. I promise I'll be exactly like him in thirty years."

"I'm holding you to that promise, but what about this case?"

"Well," Wilfred said, "Leber is, as you know, one of the most thoughtful individuals I have ever encountered. He sent a memo about the matter—-which, by the way, they're calling The Puppet's Case—-to a number of judges in the Constitutional Court, some key members of the Bundestag, the Bundesrat, and to a number of cabinet ministers."

"Must be something very important going on with your Mr. Puppet."

"Oh. I forgot. Leber also sent his memo to heads of the German military."

"My God, what does this puppet character want?"

"To be thrown in jail for the rest of his life," he told her.

"Wilfred, how big a threat is this man that it takes the Court, an act of the legislature, and every soldier in the country to put him behind bars?"

Wilfred laughed. "It's a long story. I'll tell you about the case another time. For now, I'll just say that Leber received a bunch of comments and came to see me privately. Our section is taking the case. He wants me to be the rapporteur for the Puppet. I'm to be that man's advocate for the judges."

"Good," she said, finishing the dishes in the sink. "As always, you'll gather the evidence, have a hearing, and write a brief for your colleagues. You'll be brilliant, as always. Is there a problem?"

"There is, but it's hard to describe. What I'm wrestling with is that Leber wants me to be scrupulously honest. He used those words, Ingrid, scrupulously honest."

"People do that all the time, Wilfred. When we make notes in a patient's chart, we're expected to be honest. Otherwise we have a patient who can suddenly be put on a wrong regimen, and we end up notifying relatives that Uncle Max is in a coma."

"It's different with The Puppet's Case," he said. "And the difference has more to do with me."

"Maybe we can talk this through tonight," she said.

"A good idea," he said, as she kissed him and left to catch her bus to work.

Finishing his coffee and toast, Wilfred thought about how perfect was her analogy concerning the charts of sick patients in the hospital. What if the world is sick, in the way that Hershel Selden says it is?

He took his dishes to the sink and started washing them. What if being honest, scrupulously honest, he thought, put him seriously at odds with colleagues and those who watch and comment on the work of the Court?

He remembered searching Leber's face for a clue as to whether the Presiding Justice meant exactly what he had said. "You know, Fritz, there are conventions of thought in our daily lives. One does not contravene those well-worn understandings without..." Wilfred hesitated, "...without consequences."

"There will only be consequences, as you say," Leber responded, "if you don't do your job exactly as your reason and judgment dictate."

Not totally convinced about the offer of unbridled freedom of expression, Wilfred probed, "Of all the judges under your supervision, why did you choose me to be the rapporteur in this case?"

Leber reached into a wide file holder he was carrying and took out two spiral bound sheaths of paper. Each one was over two hundred pages in length. Wilfred recognized them immediately.

"A young man in college wrote these two theses. They're titled *History as Folly* and *Where Folly is likely to Lead.* You remember those pieces of work?

"Of course."

"Do you stand by them both?"

"Without reservation," the young judge said.

"So," said Leber, "when I was figuring out who might be the Puppet's rapporteur, I wanted a judge who had a grasp of history that in some way matched the tragic, sorrowful turns that history has taken. I wanted a judge who had an imagination that could envision a role that our Constitutional Court here in Karlsruhe might undertake to possibly correct some of those sorrowful mistakes."

Leber put both theses on Wilfred's desk. "Brush up, and get to work. I have your back. Understood?"

"Clearly," Wilfred said, shaking hands with Leber. After the Presiding Judge left, Wilfred slowly and carefully read both papers, including the footnotes. When he'd finished, he had the clear understanding that his boss wanted him to put aside fears of criticism. He had just been asked to disregard all conventions in thinking that stood in the way of truth. He'd been given a rare freedom that few people experience. His job had just become to seek truths that elude the careful searchers who monitor their thoughts and their words to match common and mistaken beliefs.

There might be storms ahead. He owed it to his wife, Ingrid, to let her know that he might be putting them both into the middle of those storms.

Chapter 15

Words streamed silky clear through an earbud: "Subject seated. Isolated corner. Audio in place. It's a go."

A man in his late 50s, wearing grey slacks, a blue blazer, and a pale orange shirt with a white open collar rose from a couch in the waiting area of the Hyatt Regency Hotel in New Brunswick and walked toward the restaurant. When he reached the table where Hershel Selden was seated alone, having just finished breakfast, he said, "You must be Hershel. Klaus Steiner, your attorney, is a close friend of mine. He asked me to say hello to you. My name is Garrett Williams."

Hershel rose to accept a handshake and motioned to Williams to be seated. "How nice," he said. "What's the latest from Steiner? It's been well over a year since I've seen him."

Williams, tanned with a short grey beard, said quietly, "Nothing I just told you, including my name, is true. When you remember this conversation, think of me as the first gentle wave."

Hershel looked around and started to get up from the table. "I would advise you to stay seated and listen." When Hershel had settled back into his chair, Williams continued. "You have set in motion what's turning out to be a rather unfortunate set of circumstances."

"Who are you?" Hershel shot back. "What gives you the right to dictate what I can and cannot do?"

Williams motioned to the waiter to be served coffee by holding up the empty cup in front of him. After it was filled and the waiter left, he said "I am part of a group that governs in a world that refuses to undertake that responsibility."

"Who do you work for?"

"A group."

"Does it have a name?"

"Names and faces change over time. The mission remains the same."

"I've heard enough nonsense. Kindly leave or I'll call for the police."

Williams, unfazed, said, "The proceedings in Karlsruhe are a threat to what we've built over the last hundred years. We would like you to bring those proceedings to a halt."

"And I'm to do that because?"

"You may wish to live out your life, with your new love, Ms. Whalen, in a place of your choice, one of ever-unfolding splendor. Let me suggest a luscious green valley in Tuscany. Servants. A budget that will allow for travel and cultural enrichment, a budget so generous that she may remain in that place, if she wishes, for the rest of her natural life or move on to another of her choice."

Hershel felt a wave of fury within him at the mention of Anne's name by this very smooth, creepy man. He fought against displaying anger. For her sake, he had to know more about him and what he was saying. "Are you with the Mossad?" Hershel demanded.

Williams waived his hand dismissively. "Mossad, CIA, MI6. All that you know or think that you know is a mirage that we've put in place so you will continue to go about your lives as we direct."

"Tuscany," Hershel said, "and generous expenses. That comes to quite a sum of money."

"It will be the equivalent," said Williams, "of a penny compared to the commerce that flows through us and around this world."

"What shall I do with the remorse that I carry?"

"As you said to Ms. Whalen at the airport, and I'm quoting exactly, 'I don't know how this will turn out, but I've done all that I can. It's up to them now.' You remember saying that, do you not, Hershel?"

Hershel fought against the urge to drive his fist into William's face. "So, I'm to just let go of my guilt?"

"Like letting go of a tiny feather into a spring breeze from your balcony and watching it float toward Livorno on the Mediterranean Sea."

When Hershel did not respond, Williams added, "And you could continue being Ms. Whalen's gardener in the soil of Tuscany. Isn't that how you referred to yourself, her gardener, when you called her from Karlsruhe to tell her of your flight information?"

"You had no right to..."

"Please understand, Mr. Selden, that we are bound by no laws."

Hershel, looking down, rubbed his chin and then his throat, as though weighing the proposal. After a moment, he said, "Of course, you would want me to direct Klaus Steiner to dismiss my application."

"Correct."

"Then I would have the idyllic life that you're describing?"

"Exactly."

"But one thought would bother me. I could never be comfortable without knowing why your group, the..."

"It has no name. We are simply business associates."

"Why would your group be so opposed to what I'm trying to do there?"

"You don't want to be asking so many questions," Williams said after the voice in his earbud said "Goodby Tuscany."

"Look," Hershel said, "we go from war to war without stopping. Unless people like me are encouraged to resist, the destruction will be endless."

Williams stiffened slightly as the earbud directed, "Wrap it up. You're looking at a dead man."

From observing the man's reaction, Hershel knew that this group, whoever they are, somehow benefits from the mayhem.

"I'm the first gentle wave," said Williams with gravity. "You have forty-eight hours to accept my proposal. If you accept, I will be involved with making your lives pleasant."

"Good," said the earbud.

"If we do not hear from you within that time, then the offer is rescinded."

"And what happens at that point?"

"Dark things that I'm not at liberty to disclose."

"Like what?"

"Thin ice," said the earbud.

"Let me just add," Williams said, "that you have a vivid imagination. Use it."

"Good. Exit," said the earbud.

Williams stood up, took a card from his coat pocket, and put it on the table in front of Hershel. It was a blank card with a shallow wavy line in the middle, done with a black pen. The underneath portion of the wavy line had been filled in with a blue marker, some quarter inch wide. Underneath the blue marker line was a telephone number with a local area code, handwritten.

A waiter came to the table with the check after Williams had left the room. "The man who was sitting here," Hershel asked, "did you ever see him before?"

"I think so," the young man said. "I don't remember his name, but I took some courses in my sophomore year when I thought I was going to major in criminal justice. I may be wrong, but I think he was one of the guest lecturers."

"So, he's a teacher?"

"No. Either a chief of police or a chief of detectives. I don't remember from where. Will that be all?" the waiter asked, putting the check down on the table next to the card with the wavy blue line.

Chapter 16

Hershel called Anne. They met in the library. To avoid being overheard, they talked while moving between book stacks and in and out of small rooms designated as quiet study areas. She listened intently, on occasion shaking her head from side to side. Their final destination was a broom closet in a hallway behind swinging doors with a sign that read Staff Only.

Leaving the broom closet door open a crack, Hershel whispered "Is it possible that Williams is just a lone lunatic?"

Anne sat down on a stepstool. She leaned forward, hugging her knees. Hershel looked outside into the hallway. Seeing no one, he put the light on in the tiny room, closed the door, and leaned against a ladder, facing her.

"He knew what we talked about on the telephone?" she asked.

"Yes."

"And he quoted our conversation at the airport verbatim?"

"No question."

"That would have taken serious eavesdropping," she said, "probably the work of many people."

"Have you been talking about the case with anyone around here recently?" Anne asked.

"No. Only briefly with one of the professors whose names you gave me. And not recently."

"So, Williams obviously knows more about what's going on in Karlsruhe than we do," Anne said

"It would seem so."

"But what's happening there," she said, "from what Steiner told you, is that the judges, for the last year and a half, are mostly talking to each other."

Hershel nodded in agreement. "His knowing what they might be leaning towards means..."

"Means more eavesdropping," Anne said, "or perhaps having an informant in Karlsruhe..."

"Or both," Hershel concluded.

Anne hesitated. "I would say it's likely this group is real. They have resources. We would be foolish not to take the threat seriously."

Anne hugged her knees harder. "Damn," she said, "we have to figure this out." She rocked back and forth. "They could have killed you on the spot. Why didn't they?"

The room was quiet. Hershel checked the hallway again. Seeing no one, he returned to the ladder. "The judges," he responded, "they're quite possibly thinking about a decision that could go against the interests of this group, whoever the hell they are."

"Okay," Anne responded. "And the judges might want to continue with the case, even if you're not around. But their efforts could be stopped if, while you're alive, you demand a dismissal."

"More than that," Hershel said. "While we're vacationing for life in Tuscany, this group can force us to issue statements along the lines that the German government is attempting to undermine the State of Israel."

"My God," said Anne, "at the same time they might try to make you into a living monster to the right-wing elements in Germany. Your lies, they would say, are proof that the Jews are trying to control their judicial system——and the world, for that matter. History has proven Hitler to be right."

"And my case," Hershel asked, "interferes with the business of Williams' group because?"

"Because they thrive on creating fear, mischief, and enemies. Those are the tools they use to exercise control, control they say they've had for how long?"

"A hundred years," said Hershel, repeating what Williams had told him.

"What the hell could he have meant," Hershel asked, "about being in control and directing affairs for a hundred years?"

Anne rocked back and forth. "It's hard to know exactly what they celebrate as a great beginning? It could be destruction of the League of Nations. Maybe it was making communism appear to be satanic at the time the Bolsheviks took power in Russia."

The two of them were quiet for a long while. Hershel broke the silence. "I don't know how to say this. But if you wanted...If you thought there's no way to stop..."

Anne put a hand up. "It's a bad deal they're offering," she said. "Add to that, we have no way of knowing that they wouldn't use us to stop the case and then murder us as soon as we did what they demanded. As Williams said, they are beyond the laws. In my opinion, they are probably also beyond all ethical constraints."

"I would never want any harm to come to you," he pleaded. "So, maybe if we think about..."

"Well, I think they're a bunch of oafs," she replied. "If they had any brains, they would have offered us an idyllic life in Dublin. Then maybe we might have taken them seriously."

Hershel laughed. Anne rose from the stool. She took his hands and pressed them to her cheek. Hershel put his arms around her and held her tightly. The two of them swayed gently, side to side, as much in thought as in the delight of being close and being safe for the moment.

"So, forty-eight hours. No, forty-six hours, and then I tell Williams to go fuck himself."

"I guess so," Anne responded. "Don't bother offering him the Dublin option."

"You know I love you very much," he said. "Whatever few hours there are remaining, I'm blessed to be sharing them with you."

"Should you be reaching out to Sarah and to your sons?"

"I don't think that's necessary. Sarah has it fixed in her mind that I'm out of my mind and a traitor. My sons see it the same way."

There was a long silence. Anne said, "I could have gotten us an invitation to visit Lambay."

"Lambay what?"

"It's an island off the coast of Ireland, a bird sanctuary."

He laughed. "But there may be no sanctuary for us," Hershel said, as they walked out of the broom closet.

"My guess," she said, "is that you're correct."

Stopping Anne before they reached the swinging doors that read Staff Only, Hershel asked, "Just what is it about my case that makes this group so adamant that they need to buy me off or kill me?"

"The way I see it," Anne said slowly, "they can maintain a fair amount of control over people's thinking and their lives, but that ability to control might vanish in an instant, in a microsecond of recognition..."

"Recognition that we've all been just puppets," Hershel concluded.

"Exactly."

Chapter 17

Wilfred Shoft stood alongside four of his fellow judges at a session of the Federal Constitutional Court. They all wore bright red robes and matching round red hats. When the Court was called to order by the clerk, they took their hats off, put them down in front of them, and sat behind a long, unadorned rostrum that was raised only slightly above the lawyers, litigants, and members of the public who sat facing them. The tables at which the lawyers sat were narrow, sparse, and light tan.

Wide windows allowed the room, on the top floor of the simple, modern courthouse building on Schlossbezirk, to be filled with natural light. The judge's chairs were beige. The low rostrum was a pale yellow. The walls were a shade or two darker, toward light orange. The floor was carpeted in low-pile light green. There was seating for some two hundred people. An overflow crowd could be accommodated by a raised gallery in the rear, several rows high.

The only embellishment in the room was the German Eagle. In pale white, it stood, in low relief, with wings outstretched, on the wall to the right of the judges as one faced them.

Visitors to the Court who were sitting near the windows viewed two very different worlds. Outside stood a dominating structure, the Karlsruhe Palace. Exuding monarchical power, it had been built with wrought iron and heavy dark bricks at a time when the people were just beginning to reach beyond feudal constraints that had been imposed upon them. Inside the courtroom was a vastly different setting, one of softness and gentle colors. A visitor sitting by the window might pray that this side of the glass will help to usher in a future of perfect order with freedom and justice for all.

The case that Wilfred and the other judges were hearing involved use of police dogs during unplanned, spontaneous demonstrations. Petitioners challenged the practice that several departments had undertaken to have leashed police dogs present at such meetings in case there might be unforeseen difficulties involving crowd control.

The petitioners had shown, by way of affidavits, that they experienced anxiety at the sight of those dogs, and that anxiety interfered with their guaranteed right of freedom to meet under Article 8 of the German Constitution. Yes, they said, police authorities must be able to use dogs when circumstances required limitations on freedom of assembly for purposes of public safety. However, their presence without any sign that they might be needed was violative of their rights.

The Justices were allowing attorneys for the petitioners to give brief oral arguments, specifically to expand on how claims of anxiety are likely to affect the outcome of public gatherings. The petitioners themselves were present and might be called to testify briefly, if it were deemed necessary by any of the Justices.

Wilfred would probably be voting in favor of the petitioners. While the lawyers spoke on their behalf, he thought about some of the steps he'd been taking as rapporteur in The Puppet's Case. For the past eighteen months, Judge Schoft, beyond keeping up with his usual calendar of cases, had been deep in the study of world history. In addition, he'd been in touch with key members of the German government concerning the case.

After informing his liaison with the Bundestag, the lower house of the German legislature, about the fact that he intended to hold hearings in the matter, there was a silence on the telephone line. "Judge Shoft," said Kurt Meyer.

"Please call me Wilfred."

"Wilfred, why are you saying that our war crime laws might be might be ineffectual? Are they not just like those being carried out at The Hague itself?"

"Yes, but what if that whole approach is near useless?"

"So, what are you asking, that we fire all the judges at The Hague and do it better ourselves?"

"I didn't say that, Kurt. It's just becoming clearer every day that the systems put in place to assure peace are broken."

"And how are you so sure of that?"

"It's a truth so stark that it's no longer deniable."

Wilfred heard a loud "humph." After a brief silence, Kurt Meyer asked, "Is Fritz Leber aware of all that you're putting together?"

"Yes, and he told me the other day that anyone who reads newspapers has to be aware that what I'm saying makes sense. I'm not being disrespectful," Wilfred added, "but what newspapers do you read?"

"Why, the *Neues Deutchland* and *Die Zeit*. And, I also catch the *New York Times* and *Le Monde* occasionally."

"Well, haven't you noticed" Wilfred responded. "that wars, war crimes, and people being uprooted by violence go on and on now without an end in sight?"

"I'm no expert in such matters."

"There's not need for experts, Kurt. Violence without end is in plain sight. Should we stick our heads in the sand and pretend that we're doing something about it, or should we look into another way to go about things that can get to the bottom of the problem?"

"I'll get back to you," Kurt replied.

The next morning, Kurt Meyer called back to say that the matter was sensitive. Perhaps the best place for an airing of the subject was indeed before the Constitutional Court in a full abstract review instead of on the floor of the Bundestag. Wilfred told Kurt that he agreed completely and went on to call his liaison at the Bundesrat, the upper house of the German legislature.

Herman Zeitz was outspoken in his opposition. "So," he shouted over the telephone, "is that little Jew puppet's tail supposed to wag the entire German government?"

Wilfred had never met Zeitz. He had no way of knowing whether the man harbored an ancient anti-Semitism, as did many people. Maybe he was overwhelmed with work or had been soldiering through a lengthy illness. Carefully,

Wilfred responded, "We, at the Court, are less interested in the personalities of the litigants than the weight of the issues that they bring us."

There was no response. The Judge continued. "The focus of the case is not him. It's us. Are we, as they say, asleep at the switch while the world seems to be headed toward warfare without end? And this is happening at a time when there is need, as never before, for peace."

"I don't know," said Zeitz.

"Kurt Meyer will be there as an observer for the Bundestag. But Herman, you know that big changes cannot happen without the approval of the Bundesrat. Your presence can be the key to a better future."

"I'll be there," said Zeitz, in a voice that sounded like a threat. "But just don't think, brother Shoft, that you can blow smoke up my ass."

"Herman," said Wilfred, "I do like to keep all of my options open."

Zeitz laughed loudly. "That's good. One of these days we will meet, you and I. Meanwhile don't get too enamored with your efforts on behalf of that strange man. What's his name? Hershel the Mighty, Ruler of Empires, and Champion of the Downtrodden?"

"I'll tell his lawyer that Selden has a new royal status."

They both laughed. Zeitz had great influence in the Bundesrat. Wilfred sensed that beneath the man's outward displays of ridicule, he understood the significance of The Puppet's Case.

But how, Wilfred pondered after his calls with Meyer and Zeitz, should he begin to portray the root causes of the endless wars and continuous savagery? Selden had pushed aside a stone that covered the opening to a cave. Light streamed to the bottom where beasts growled. Wilfred shuddered. This will not be easy.

Chapter 18

"That was four days ago," Hershel said, after telling his nephew, Alan, about his encounter with the man who said he was Garrett Williams. The telephone on Alan's desk rang. He answered and told his secretary that there were to be no calls.

"Holy shit," the nephew said, as he rose from his desk and looked out his office window, thinking he might see his uncle's pursuers on nearby rooftops in downtown New Brunswick. "Did you call the police?"

"No."

"Why the hell not?"

"He might be a policeman himself."

"That doesn't mean," Alan said, "that he can commit the crimes of extortion and threatening murder."

"But if he's connected to law enforcement, he might be able to know within minutes if a man named Selden signed a criminal complaint against him in this city. Alan, that complaint could result in them murdering me before an investigation could even begin."

"And before you even started the process," Alan added, "of making an identification of this Williams guy."

"Exactly."

"What are you going to do?" Alan asked.

"I spoke to Klaus Steiner and asked him if he needed anything further from me. Steiner said that my depositions and statements were adequate for now. I was just to wait and we would see what might develop."

"Did you tell him about the threat by Williams?"

"No."

"Why not?"

"Because I had to assume that those thugs would be listening in on the call, and I didn't think Steiner could be of help with them."

Alan came back to the desk and lowered himself slowly into the high-backed leather chair. Staring at his uncle, he asked, "Do you think we're being overheard right now?"

"No. I came to your office without making an appointment. I was the last person to get onto a crowded elevator. I exited several floors above yours and walked down to get here. We can talk freely. And I came here because there's something very important that I need you to do for me."

"Tell me. What can I do?"

"Try to reach me once a day. If you can't, and I have not called you, please assume that I've been abducted and possibly murdered."

Hershel grabbed the back of his neck and looked down before continuing. "If I'm found dead, look into the cause of my death, no matter how things appear." After a pause, "Don't believe the truth of any suicide note that may be found."

The two of them stared at one another, as though Hershel had transported them both to another realm where language was useless and events cascaded about without making sense.

Hershel broke the silence. "Get in touch with Steiner right away if anything happens."

Alan nodded.

"And tell him that my final wish was that the case go forward without me, no matter what anyone else may be saying about my intentions."

After a short time of silence, Hershel asked, "Is that enough? My word to you?"

"No," Alan said, after giving the question some thought. He called his secretary in and dictated a brief description of the encounter between Williams and

Hershel. Hershel signed the document, and his signature was notarized. The last sentence read: "It is my wish to have The Puppet's Case continue beyond my death, in spite of any statements alleged to have been made by me or extorted from me to the contrary before my death."

After the document was completed, the two men sat alone in Alan's office. Alan asked, "Why is your matter called The Puppet's Case?"

"The German courts try to give anonymity to litigants. When possible, cases are referred to by a pseudonym or a catchphrase. I am The Puppet."

"Uncle, that would be my least likely name for you. To me you were always a hero, a two-fisted guy who didn't shy away from whatever had to be done."

Hershel paused, trying to think through how best to respond to his nephew. "Alan, you always refer to me as a strong man."

"That's because you are."

"Listen, your making me into a hero is like taking a medicine that helps you deal with the fact that not enough of us resisted, street-by-street and house-by-house, when we could have."

Alan started to react to that statement and then stopped himself. Hershel continued, "Yes, we were puppets back then when we allowed ourselves to be rounded up, but I was no less of a puppet when I murdered innocent Arabs in 1948."

"You were fighting for your life."

"Yes, no question, but in the larger picture I was just a puppet again. Alan, real strength is having the courage to see the truth."

"The truth?"

"The Americans were in charge then, but they didn't give a crap if we lived or died. We dutifully came into the arena, Arabs and Jews, and we tore at each other's throats, forgetting what was really at stake."

"Uncle, I think you may be," he hesitated, "under great strain."

"No. I was there in 1948. People didn't think much of Palestine being a British protectorate under rules set up by the League of Nations, but it was...it was something. An effort..."

"That came to nothing," Alan said.

"It came to nothing because our new acquaintances, Garrett Williams and his group, wanted no interference. They were busy inventing and selling Cold

War hatreds against the Russians. The very last thing they wanted at that time was effective international governing. Peace became impossible. It was just puppets fighting puppets, and we Jews were hypnotized into thinking that was wonderful. We won, and now we're showing the world."

"Yes," Alan said, "showing the world that we remember the Holocaust, and we're saying every day: Never again. Never again."

"Nephew, that phrase is just another dose of the medicine that you like to take. Militance is a drug. At best, all it can do is bring short term relief. Using the mantra of never again, instead of searching for a better way forward can only lead, in the end, to destruction."

"A better way...?"

"Yes. Real strength is finding a way toward peace with justice based on brotherhood between Jews and Arabs. That's the search for a better way forward."

"I'm sorry, Uncle, but you're dreaming."

"It's better to search for a path than to do nothing in the face of this nightmare that's been foisted upon us. Garrett Williams' group created and profits from permanent war in the world. The fuel that they use now for permanent war is the existence of terrorism. And they keep terrorism alive every day through an unsettled Palestine, along with drone strikes and acts of war against Muslims in dozens of countries around the world. Alan, in all this wholesale lawlessness, we are the puppets that keep their coffers filled. And all we say, again and again, is only what the ventriloquist allows us to say: Never again. Never again."

The two men sat quietly. "So that's why you're so intent on this case?" Alan asked.

"Yes, we can be warriors. Brave characters who shout out how strong we are, but Alan, if that's all we do, then we Jews miss the point of the spiritual journey all of us must take toward justice and peace."

Alan walked Hershel out of his office and checked out the hallway. There was no one waiting nearby. He pushed the button for the elevator. It was empty, and Hershel took it to the third floor so that he could walk the remaining flights to ground level. Peeking through the door into the lobby, nothing looked amiss.

IMPASSE

A short distance after Hershel walked out the front door of the office building into a crisp winter day, a man in a brown suit quietly said, "Contact. East on foot. Sandford Street."

His earbud demanded: "Image."

Brown suit accommodated by taking a confirming photograph of Hershel. Several moments later, a van was directed, "A hundred yards. Proceed. Door open." The final command was "It's a go. Take up."

Three men approached Hershel. One grabbed his feet, another, his chest. A third put tape over the old man's mouth. In seconds, Hershel was in the van. A drug was administered through needle-stick in his neck by a fourth person who had been waiting in the van. They held Hershel until he went limp. The van headed out onto Route 27, northbound.

Hershel drifted gently into a quiet, brilliant sunshine. A backyard in Wurzburg. His mother was taking laundry off the clothesline and placing it carefully into a basket. When she picked up the basket, she hefted it to her face and breathed in the warmth of the sun, essences of flowers, and the aroma of rich soil under foot, all of which had gathered on the sheets, pillowcases, and towels. She smiled and then looked down at Hershel before swinging the basket around and heading for the house. Young Hershel tried to tell her something, but didn't know what to say or how to say it.

And then, he and Solveg, his childhood girlfriend, were running on cobblestone streets. They ran past fence posts and farms with crops and animals. With a church in the distance, they veered off the road and came to a forest. Standing with Solveg on a soft bed of pine needles, Hershel tried to tell the girl something, but words refused to gather. He only smiled. She smiled back. Neither of them was tired. Both of them knew they had a special bond that would be with them always.

As Hershel dreamed on, he was carried from the van into an airport hanger and onto an airplane. The injections continued. An ocean slid by beneath the aircraft, as did another continent to the east. Another hanger. A swift, dark limousine. Then a room with shades drawn. Hershel open his eyes and tried to wipe away teary dampness from them, but his arms were lashed down to the sides of his bed. His ankles were bound, as well. For a short while, he tried to fathom what might have occurred, and then he remembered.

Chapter 19

Hershel lay still with his eyes closed as he heard a door open and close. He felt someone releasing the straps that held his arms down. "You've been a very busy man." Hershel kept his eyes closed and said nothing. The man untied the straps around his ankles.

"That's more than enough sleep," the man said, as he pushed a button on the hospital bed, stopping when Hershel was near a sitting position. Hershel opened his eyes. The man looked to be in his forties, was well-tanned and muscular. He wore a short-sleeved brown shirt, open at the collar, and khaki pants. His sharp features were accentuated by a close-cropped, military style haircut.

"Who are you?"

"Manolo."

"Just Manolo?"

"Let's get right to business," the man said impatiently.

"Where am I?"

"You're in the one country in the world that reached out for your little ass when none of the others gave a shit. Does that answer your question?"

Hershel looked around. The room seemed to be part of a hospital. Next to his bed was a tall post that held an intravenous drip bag. Next to that was a stand with a sleeve used to measure blood pressure. Window blinds were closed.

Looking down, he saw that he'd been put into a hospital gown. A steel locker stood on the wall opposite his bed, next to a sink with a supply of liquid soap, paper towels, tissues, and latex gloves.

"This is not a hospital. You're too sick even for hospitals," Manolo said, circling the side of his own head with his right index finger. "Now, you listen to me, and listen carefully. Do I have your full attention?"

"Are you Israeli Intelligence?" Hershel shot back.

Manolo hovered over Hershel. With a raised voice and taut facial muscles, he said "Let's just put me in the category of soldier, and I'm losing patience with you, asshole." Manolo continued. "Yesterday, you texted a message to your wife. You told her that you have not been well. You're sorry to have caused such a fuss. You were confused. You're coming home."

"I never..."

"Shut up. A man fitting your description and carrying your passport boarded a commercial flight which landed in Israel this morning. He disembarked and disappeared. You will enter your homeland by walking out that door. A car will take you from here to your house. A reporter has already called Sarah. She told the reporter that you had not been well but have come to your senses. The reporter asked about your case. Whatever case you were involved with, your wife said, should be ended. And that's what you want to happen at this time."

"My God," said Hershel.

"You arrive home, kiss your wife, and confirm the story when the reporter asks."

"And what do you hope to accomplish by this charade?"

"Your new friends in Germany will be unsteady about taking your assertions seriously, coming from a sick man who now says he's been delusional all along."

"And if I don't go along with this?"

"An old man, on his way home, has a heart attack. The last anyone knows about him is that he sent a message to his good wife about what a fool he had been. End of story. A funeral. Wonderful orations about your life as war hero. And, yes, like many soldiers, you had difficulties with what's now called post traumatic stress syndrome. In lieu of flowers, the family would appreciate donations to the Soldier's Spirit Foundation, a group that's dedicated to helping men and women who served in the armed forces and now need a little help themselves."

"You're not Israeli."

"No."

"Why are you doing this?"

"Look, shit-for-brains, this was all laid out for you."

"You mean Garrett Williams? What he told me?"

"Williams, yes, but I don't waste my breath the way he does. Look, jerkoff, it took a long time and a boat-load of effort to put everything in place. We're not about to let some stupid-ass judges in Germany go poking around into the way things get settled now."

"You mean unsettled," Hershel said "unsettled is what you do, like having Arabs and Jews kick the shit out of one another while..."

"Shut the fuck up," Manolo shouted. "Your suit is in the locker. Shower, shave, and get into it. The car leaves in an hour. You'll either be in the back with me doing what I tell you or you'll be in the trunk, dead."

Hershel started to get up. Manolo went to steady him. The older man pushed his arm away. Hershel stood and leaned on the IV pole, as he walked into the bathroom that had no door. While showering, he thought about how cruel it was for these men to have given Sarah the false hope that he was coming home and all would be as it had been. Nothing was beyond them. Nothing.

"Nothing," Hershel said, as he was coming out of the shower.

"Talking to yourself?" Manolo mused. "Good. I'll write that in your chart."

Hershel toweled himself dry and began to shave. Manolo moved a chair into the entrance of the bathroom and sat watching the old man's every move. The bathroom was windowless. Before sitting, Manolo opened the thumbsnap over a revolver he carried in a belt holster.

"So, I have choices to make?" he asked. "If I say screw you, you kill me outright with some drug that stops my heart?"

"Right. It's a sure pop. Takes a minute or two and you're gone."

"What if I go home, tell Sarah everything, and then let the reporters know who and what you people are, blood sucking monsters?"

"Good question. Right now, there are microphones all over your old lady's place. We know everything she says. We know when she farts. There's nothing you can say to her that we won't hear. And wherever you take her outside, there are directional microphones from several vantage points that will pick up every word."

Hershel shook his head to acknowledge that he understood and continued shaving.

"Understanding how confused your mind has become," Manolo said, "let me make the picture clearer for you. We don't just have directional microphones, we have snipers in place who can shoot the nipple off a tit at three hundred yards. And we have reporters who will spin the story that you got what you deserved. Any more questions?"

"Just one. How do you sleep at night?"

"I'm good at my job," Manolo said, irritated as though the question made no sense. "So, my family is secure. My wife and children have the best," with emphasis on "the best."

Hershel put the razor down and washed the soap off his face. He went to the locker to get dressed. Manolo, keeping a constant watch over his prisoner, said "I sleep at night like a baby, whether you sleep, die, or piss your life away."

The front door opened. Someone handed Manolo an envelope. He opened it, removed a passport, and put it into an inside suit jacket pocket in the locker while Hershel was slowly getting his socks on.

Chapter 20

Manolo motioned for Hershel to walk out the front door. It was near noon. Hershel shielded his eyes from the bright sunshine. The building he'd been in looked like any one of a dozen houses on the block. Hershel remembered the term safe house from a novel he'd read. In front of the safe house were three vehicles. All were light grey in color. Three men were standing near the cars. The car in the middle was larger than the others. Hershel guessed that the one in the middle was to transport him.

He assumed that the three men were high-level security people, good at their jobs, and capable of assessing risks and requirements to deal with those risks. With that in mind, Hershel quietly and slowly went to one knee, as though he were about to faint and had the wherewithal to let himself down slowly.

Manolo hurried over and raised the old man up slowly, looking at his face for signs of illness. Seeing none, he walked Hershel toward the back seat on the driver's side of the car in the middle. Hershel made sure that his steps were slow and measured. Without looking up to notice, he was sure he had given the impression intended. This prisoner required no special attention. Age had rendered him near helpless. This job was a walk in the park.

Manolo opened the rear door as the three drivers were entering their vehicles. Before Hershel got in, he looked at the small lever that's used as a safety lock so that children in the back seats could not open the doors from the inside.

Open. It was open, not locked. Hershel mumbled a thank you to God as he struggled to get his legs in, appearing to need help from Manolo.

Manolo walked around the back of the car and opened the rear door on the other side. Before seating himself next to Hershel, Hershel heard the thumb-snap made when Manolo secured his revolver into the gun holster. Yes, thought Hershel. Another second. A blessed second. He had no choice but to try an escape. Compared to all of the other outcomes, death by a bullet in the back was preferable by far.

Hershel guessed that they were a short distance from Jerusalem. Good security would require that they be left with only a short drive. He estimated that this small town must be within ten, perhaps twenty minutes of their destination.

The cars started moving slowly through crowded and winding streets. Hershel prayed that they would hit some sort of significant congestion before reaching a major highway and attaining high speed. A moment later, around a bend to the left, an area used by street vendors on both sides came into view.

As the vehicles slowed to a few miles per hour, Hershel cupped his right hand and slammed his open fist against Manolo's eyes, blinding the man momentarily. With his left hand, Hershel opened the car door and jumped out, leaving the door wide open. And just as he had hoped, the driver of the car in which he had been riding jammed on the brakes, stopping immediately. Hershel hit the ground, lay flat, and quickly moved himself under the trunk portion of his stopped car as the vehicle that followed stopped immediately behind.

If one of the drivers had seen him drop down and go under the vehicle, Hershel could expect to die. It would be a good death, he said to himself, a soldier's death, as he spidered his way toward food vendors on the right side of the road. Not looking back to see whether he had pursuers, Hershel stayed low by crawling between the stalls in the direction of what appeared to be a warren of ancient houses on tiny alleyway streets. By now, his pursuers were on the opposite side, weapons drawn, shouting, and upsetting carts of food in their search for the escaped prisoner.

When Hershel was behind the walls of buildings, he began to run slowly through the narrow, winding streets. Not having had time to warm up and stretch, he started at quarter speed and prayed that he wouldn't cramp up and be forced to stop. After a minute, he was able to pick up the pace. The training regimen that included his running up the steps of the Rutgers football stadium allowed Hershel to maintain a steady three-quarter speed pace. His breathing and heart rate, following the exertion of crawling under the car and through the stalls, had normalized. Now, it was a question of whether he could maintain that pace and find a place of safety.

Hearing a motor scooter behind him, Hershel stopped and turned around. The driver looked to be a young man in his twenties wearing a T-shirt with a logo for a brand of sneakers. Hershel held his thumb up, asking for a ride. As the scooter got closer, he changed from a thumbs up signal to holding his hands together upright in the universal sign of prayer.

The driver braked and motioned for him to get on. Hershel quickly climbed aboard. As the young man headed away from the area, Hershel looked back. There was no commotion in the streets immediately behind them. There were no pursuers to be seen. Fearing for the safety of the boy who had picked him up, Hershel tried to imagine whether the young man could have been identified. Were there cameras in the area? Helicopters above? A drone hovering? Were there agents on the side streets? It appeared unlikely that the boy was in any danger. But the longer they stayed on those streets, the more likely it was that someone would connect the blue-suited escapee with that youngster. So, after they'd been riding for some five minutes through sparsely crowded winding back roads, Hershel tapped him on the back and motioned to be let off. The young man stopped. Hershel jumped off and ducked into an alleyway between old houses. He saluted the driver. The boy smiled and saluted back as he drove off.

Hershel saw a clothesline and then another. He quickly removed his suit and white shirt, throwing them over the place where he saw an old pair of slacks and a pullover sleeved shirt that looked to be his size. He walked out of the alley without, to his knowledge, having been observed. Turning in the direction that the boy had been traveling, Hershel walked slowly, stopping at what looked like an Arab's shop, to buy a hat with as wide a brim as the selection allowed.

When he took his wallet out to pay for the hat, he panicked. Had he been left with only American dollars? Would having only dollars in this out of the way neighborhood connect him to the escape? To his relief, the cash he had when he was kidnapped had been changed to Israeli shekels. Whoever the hell those bastards are, he thought, those owners of the universe, they were obviously thorough. The shopkeeper, a young woman, hardly looked up from the book she was reading to take payment in the currency of the country and give change to the old man who looked like any one of thousands of old men who lived in and worked in the area.

Hershel walked to a café and sat in the back, watching the street. Over coffee and biscuits, he considered his options. He had to get out of this area, quickly and without being noticed. Not easily done, he thought, with roads that contained checkpoints and an identity on his passport that made him a target for assassination. Hershel knew exactly where he needed to go, but a safe way to get there eluded him.

Chapter 21

Alan Selden sat across the desk from Klaus Steiner. It was late afternoon in Karlsruhe. Steiner, with his tie loosened, signed the mail he'd generated from dictation through the day. "Take your time," said Selden, understanding a lawyer's need to proofread carefully at the end of a workday.

When Steiner had finished and signed the last letter, he took the pile out to his secretary, thanked her, and came back to his office. Closing the door behind him, he asked, "How can you be so sure?"

"I'm one hundred percent positive because I went to the airport. It wasn't easy. Had to call in a favor from the Chief of Police in Newark. They let me look at the all the people who boarded El Al flights to Israel."

Steiner came back to sit in his chair. Alan leaned forward on the opposite side of the desk with both hands spread wide, as if to pounce. "The man who boarded the flight to Israel, using Hershel's identity," he said, "was not my uncle. Do you know what that means?"

In the silence that followed, Alan slowly sat back. The two men seemed to stare at the center of the desk in front of them, as though a play had been taking shape, a play that was informing them both of looming truths.

Alan continued. "And could you or anyone you know get reporters to file stories, without confirmation, based solely on an email message?"

"Did the wife, Sarah, I think that's her name, did she contact the newspapers about Hershel being in touch with her?"

"No. All she did was prepare for his return by letting the family know to be ready. Then, when he did not come through the door as expected, she called me to ask if I knew something. I told her I thought that Hershel had been kidnapped."

"He could be anywhere," said Steiner.

"My guess," Alan replied, "is that he's in Israel. The bastards would have tried to get him to go home, just as they had set it all up to happen. And maybe he's not going along with their shit plan, just as he declined a life of leisure in Italy that they offered him."

"So, if he continues to refuse to go along..."

"They will snuff out his life as easily as killing a fly with one wing."

Steiner picked up the phone and buzzed his secretary. "Please call Frederick Egon's office. Tell them I must speak to Egon personally, as soon as possible." He put the phone down slowly.

Several minutes later, the phone rang. Steiner picked it up and said, "Thanks for getting right back to me, Freddie. I'm calling about The Puppet. His nephew is in my office right now. Have you been keeping up with the twists and turns that case is making?"

"Somewhat."

"Recently," said Steiner, "a newspaper story was published in both Israel and Germany that Hershel has recanted his plea of guilty and is asserting that he was mentally unbalanced when you took his deposition."

"Yes. I heard about that."

"Well, it appears that the story is absolutely false. May I put you on speaker?"

"Of course."

"Thank you," said Steiner, as he pushed the button that brought the presence of the Attorney General into the room.

After introductions, Steiner told Egon of Hershel's meeting with a man who called himself Garrett Williams, Alan's conversation with his uncle before he went missing, and the fact that someone posing as Hershel flew to Israel, using his passport.

When Steiner completed his report, Egon asked Alan if all of what the lawyer had just said was accurate. "Every detail," replied Alan.

"The information that's circulating here in Germany is all based on planted rumors," said Steiner. "I'll be back to you when I know more, Freddie. Thanks for taking my call. I know you must be in the middle of a thousand things. I'll be in touch with you."

With that, Steiner ended the call and turned to Alan. "Stay in contact with the family in Israel. They're likely to be the best source of information. When you have anything further, come right to my office. Don't bother making an appointment."

Steiner rose from his chair and ushered Alan out of his office. When Alan started to speak, Steiner put an index finger to his own lips to stop what conversation might have ensued.

"I'll walk you to the elevator," the lawyer said. As they waited for the doors to open, Steiner leaned close to Alan and whispered, "Come back in the late afternoon tomorrow. Between now and then, buy a cheap cell phone, but don't use it. Stop at a couple of cyber cafes. Speak softly to one or two young people. Visit a library, even briefly. Got it?" Alan nodded, thanked Steiner, and walked onto the elevator.

Steiner left the office that day the way he'd left his office every day for the past thirty years. With a newspaper under his arm and carrying an attaché case, he said "good evening" to young clerks still at work. Seeing that the button had been pushed for his parking level floor, he cheerfully said, "Take me home," to the woman in the elevator standing closest to the panel of buttons.

On his way toward home, Steiner stopped at a busy mall with numerous shops, restaurants, and a movie theater. He bought a loaf of bread from an upscale boulangerie and a wedge of Camembert from a cheese shop. Packages in hand, he slowly walked to the other side of the mall and exited onto a street that ran parallel to where he had parked his car. Hailing a taxi, Steiner quickly got in, whispered the address, and asked the driver to go as fast as the law allowed.

The driver nodded. In a few moments, with no cars following the taxi, he stopped. Steiner paid the fare and was inside the Offices of the Attorney General within moments. Being known by security helped him get to Egon's personal secretary without waiting. Steiner was relieved to find out that the Attorney General was still in the building.

After telling the secretary that he must see Mr. Egon immediately, that it was an extremely urgent matter, the lawyer sat down to catch his breath and collect his thoughts.

"Why the hell didn't you just call me back?" Frederick Egon said, as he was walking toward Steiner.

"Couldn't. Is there a secure place for us to talk?"

Egon led Steiner into a windowless communications center. Computers sat in the middle of the room. Around the walls were cabinets for equipment and information storage. In one corner was a steel desk and two chairs. The two men sat across from one another in that room.

"My guess," said Egon, "is that this room will be fine."

Chapter 22

"Now, what the hell's going on here?" Egon asked.

"My client has been abducted."

"Yes. You said that during our phone call."

"And I suspect he's still alive. But to keep him from being murdered, we'll have to act quickly."

"How do you know all this?"

"Look, they could have killed him at any time. But killing him wouldn't necessarily make The Puppet Case go away. They need him to recant, publicly, and say that he was crazy to even think that he'd done anything wrong. Under those circumstances, the Judges here in Karlsruhe would think twice about going forward. Doesn't that make sense, Freddie?"

Egon pushed his chair back and took a deep breath. "I agree," he said, "but why all this," he stopped and looked around at their isolated surroundings, "need for security?"

"When we were on the phone earlier today, it dawned on me that the bastards were listening."

"Christ," said Egon.

"It's a different world now, a fucking spytopia. Privacy is gone. Every call, everywhere, is routed, analyzed, and stored."

"And calls related to The Puppet?" Egon asked.

"They would be a first priority for them because Selden's case goes to the heart of the control mechanisms that they've put in place."

"So, you're suggesting, are you not, that you need a call back of some kind?"

"Exactly. Tomorrow, at 1:00 p.m.," Steiner said.

"And give them something that will have them think twice before they murder Selden."

"Yes. It would be best, Freddie, if you could, using encrypted messages or super-secure lines, get approvals from the Chancellor's Office as well as from key legislative leaders."

"Tall order, Klaus. That's not much time."

"I don't think Selden has much time before his execution."

Egon folded his hands, thinking through who he must speak to and the conversations that needed to take place. Steiner looked on, folded his hands, and nodded slightly as a quiet token of support.

When Egon looked up at Steiner, Steiner said, "He is, you know, a citizen of Germany. That's not just bullshit words in the Constitution."

Egon nodded. Steiner continued, "They've kidnapped a German citizen and moved him illegally across borders of sovereign nations, all without due process. They're trying, by fraud, to get our Court to dismiss a case that may have important implications for justice and proper governance in this world. What they're doing right now, if they get away with it, will be a setback to our efforts here in Germany to address and stop the contagion of unending wars and war crimes around the world."

In less than fifteen minutes, Steiner was back at the mall from which he had taken a cab. He entered the mall and walked slowly through it toward the area where he had parked his car, remembering to stop and gaze in an art gallery.

He cursed the watchers and the listeners and the need to be so careful. Rather than blessedly living in the moment through a consciousness focused from within, he was now forced to observe himself from distant angles, always assessing what others might think of his actions. Words now required weighing before being uttered. Thought, itself, so burdened by defending against phantom charges of misbehavior, seemed to suddenly be an endangered activity. When, he asked himself, had this damn yoke been placed upon our lives?

Steiner watched himself slowly walk into a shop that did picture framing. A woman he took to be the owner was working at a large table, centering a mat over a photograph of a young girl riding a horse. He smiled at the woman. She smiled back and invited him to look around. The wall behind the woman was filled with samples of frames and swatches of mats. On the other walls were prints and photographs. All were framed, and all were for sale. Steiner allotted himself two minutes to be seen observing the pictures. Then he would move on, go to his car, drive home, and be finished with the game of watching himself as others might be seeing him.

He found himself staring at a print of a familiar old painting. Soldiers with rifles, bayonets attached, were shooting rows of lined-up unarmed civilians.

The woman, grey haired and looking up over her reading glasses, said "That's Goya. It's called *The Third of May 1808*."

"The soldiers?" asked Steiner.

"Napoleon's best."

"And the citizens?"

"From Madrid. Caught in the middle. They favored their own monarch."

Steiner stared at the picture, then looked around the store and outside into the mall area. No one seemed to be watching or listening. "I wonder," he said, nearly whispering, to the store owner, "how Goya would handle making a picture of an American, sitting in a trailer someplace safe in the middle of his country, pushing a button that sends a drone strike down, killing a dozen people in Pakistan who were in the middle of planning nothing more dangerous than dinner with cousins."

The shop owner stopped working on the framing of the photograph. She stood up straight and stared at Steiner. "I know Goya. Studied him in school."

Steiner drew closer to the table she was working at so that the woman would not have to raise her voice. "And he would depict the event as..."

"The sky on fire," she said, interrupting him. "Mountains running with dark blood into rivers. People cowed under pieces of the bodies that had been blown apart, trying to protect the children, who, it was clear, could never again delight in moving about freely under the sun."

"The trailer?" asked Steiner, "Would that be in the picture?"

"Most certainly. In the lower right hand corner, instead of a signature. That's where Goya would have painted the trailer, with its antenna. That would have been his way of saying here's the newest monster, capable of destroying the last vestiges of normal human expectations."

Chapter 23

Hershel sat in the very back of the bus, next to a window, feigning sleep. His clothes were a good match to the other riders, Arabs traveling into Jerusalem. There were two checkpoints. At the one closest to the city, he saw an Israeli soldier signaling for the driver to come to a full stop and open the door to the bus. Another soldier entered the bus at that stop and started walking slowly up the isle.

Huddled in the rear, Hershel considered the possibility that these soldiers had been commandeered by Manolo's group to find him. Hadn't Garrett Williams been a police officer in the United States? Listening in on his call from Karlsruhe to Anne probably involved a high level NSA security clearance. And flying him across national borders as though he were nothing more than a crate of oranges was brazen.

When the soldier was midway toward the back, Hershel gathered spit in his mouth. He let his head fall to the side away from the window and opened his mouth in a way that he imagined distorted his face. He felt a trickle of saliva wetting his jaw and moving down to his neck. His heart raced as he kept his eyes gently closed. He prayed that disgust would register high in that soldier's mind, enough to overcome an effort to identify a slovenly, unclean, sleeping Arab as the blue-suited man he might have been directed to find.

The bus began to move forward, Hershel slowly opened his eyes. The soldier was gone. Outside the window, the streets of Jerusalem, familiar places, came into view.

It took nearly an hour, walking slowly on back streets, for him to reach the small building where Julia Pozar had her office. She, the psychologist working with Avey Maisel, the lawyer, had kept Hershel from being labeled insane and drugged for the rest of his days. Julia was now his hope to remain alive. But, as he neared the front of her building, he feared that Manolo's people were near. Wouldn't they know of her work on his behalf? Were they watching now, as he stood at a nearby kiosk, looking at newspapers and magazines in a rack?

It was the end of the business day. The kiosk was busy with customers. Out of the corner of his eye, he saw Julia buying a newspaper. She tucked the newspaper under her arm, turned in his direction, and dropped a coin. Bending over to pick it up while still moving towards him, she put a key into his hand and whispered her apartment address, "83A Sofer."

As she said those words, her eyes looked straight ahead in the direction she was walking. Her hair, parted in middle, looked greyer than when Hershel had seen her last. He turned back to the newspapers and magazines, softly saying her address several times to burn it into his memory. He knew the street and mapped out a route in his mind that would take him there without walking on major thoroughfares.

As evening shadows grew long, Hershel approached Julia's apartment complex. Hers was a modest looking place on the first floor. The door faced the street. He put the key in the lock. It turned. He opened the door and quickly let himself in. Julia was in the kitchen, cooking their dinner. They hugged a quiet hello. Julia fought back a tear. "You've gotten yourself into some trouble, I see."

"Just a little," he said, laughing. "But how did you know to look for me?"

"My office is next to the men's bathroom. Normally, I don't hear anything, but today someone was shouting about what he's going to do to that puppet bastard when he gets a hold of him. I knew he was talking about you."

"That was Manolo."

"The newspaper story about you didn't sound right, so I concluded that those people were waiting for you to show up at my office."

"And your passing me the key?"

"I was looking for you on my way home, and there you were at the kiosk."

"Thank you. That's the second time you saved my life. If I had bumbled around there any longer, they would have surely caught me."

Earbuds outside Julia's office crackled, "I'm waiting. I'm waiting." It was Manolo's voice.

"Negative," replied a young man on a bicycle.

"Nothing," came from a woman with her hands on a four-wheeled shopping cart with bags of groceries.

"Same," said a man in a runner's outfit, stretching his hamstring muscles.

"I want facial recognition in place, now," was the urgent reply, "and a kill on sight. First sight." There was crackling as the broadcast was expanded to include all agents in the area. "Then grab a kid. Any fucking Arab kid will do. Throw the kid on top of that shit little Jew, and set off a bomb for the two of them, like the kid did it. A twofer. Understand? Is that so fucking hard to do? Goddamn it!"

The next day, at 1:00 p.m., Klaus Steiner, sitting in Frederick Egon's office, wiped his brow with a handkerchief as the phone rang. "Put her through," Egon said.

"Carla, it's wonderful to hear from you. Is Eric well? And the children?" Steiner recognized the voice. It was Carla Dorin, Chief-of-staff, to the Chancellor.

"That's great," Egon replied.

After a short time of listening, he said, "Irma's poetry is beginning to attain some stature. Yes...Yes... The kids?... No. When I talk about law in the house, you should see their eyes glaze over."

"To what do I owe this call?" he asked.

Egon listened and nodded to Steiner. After a short while, he said, "May I put you on speaker? Just by coincidence, the man's lawyer happens to be in my office right now. I'm sure he would want to know this, and he can answer any question you may have at this time."

Frederick pushed the speaker button. "Carla Dorin, this is Klaus Steiner."

"Mr. Steiner," she said, "may I ask a favor of you before continuing?"

"Certainly."

"What I'm about to say to Frederick involves personal communications between the Chancellery and the leadership of the Bundestag. You may be part of the conversation on the condition that you do not disclose what is said. Do you understand that? Can you abide by that?"

"Yes," stammered Klaus, "of course."

"Very well," Carla responded. "Frederick, my office has been in touch with Wilford Shoft, the rapporteur for The Puppet's Case. He tells me any assertion that Hershel Selden is not of sound mind is likely to be false. Mr. Steiner, would that be your understanding, as well?"

"Without question," Klaus said.

"Frederick, when Mr. Selden did not show up at his wife's home, our agents in Israel were told that a man who looked somewhat like him used Selden's passport to gain entry into Israel. Is that correct, Mr. Steiner?"

"Confirmed," said Steiner. "He was kidnapped in the United States, and the man you're describing boarded a plane using Hershel's identification."

"What we have is rendition, gentlemen. The norms of law and the rights of litigants are being disregarded as though they never existed."

There was a long pause. "What do you suggest we do?" Egon asked.

"The people who did this have stripped a German citizen of his most basic rights." Carla Dorin paused.

"I have directed," she continued, "Wilford Shoft to continue the litigation and put evidence of the rendition into the record. And I'm requesting you, Frederick, to begin piecing together prosecutions of all those who have been complicit in the abduction, rendition, and possibly the murder of Hershel Selden. Every one of those individuals, because they've stood in the way of a prosecution concerning war crimes, is guilty themselves of an obstruction of justice. Do you fully appreciate the gravity of this situation, Frederick?"

"I do," the Attorney General replied. "May I have the services of all necessary security agencies?"

"I've put that in the works already," Carla replied. "Good day, gentlemen. The Chancellor wishes to be updated regularly."

"Thank you," Klaus and Frederick said in unison, as Egon ended the call.

From a distant location came this call for a conference: "Collection point data analyst HQPT requests conference. Repeat. Collection point data analyst HQPT requests conference. Data gathering begun."

Chapter 24

Avey Maisel sat in the waiting area of the U.S. Consular Services Office in Jerusalem. Angular, dark skinned, and athletic, he bolted out of his small plastic seat every ten minutes and went to the windows looking toward the street. He imagined that his client, Hershel Selden, would be walking toward the building any moment now. It was near two o'clock in the afternoon. There were few cars on the roadway and none in the circular driveway out front.

It had been years since he saw Hershel. Avey remembered how thankful the man had been at being released from a psychiatric holding order. Hershel called Avey and Julia, his guardian angels and took them out to a grand dinner before going off to the United States.

The newspaper articles that said Hershel was sorry about his efforts to plead guilty to a wartime offense and that he had been depressed made no sense to Avey. Meeting with the man, here at the Consular Services Office, would clear matters up quickly.

Julia Pozar had gone to his office early that day and found out he would be in court that morning. She sat down on the bench next to him. "Look straight ahead," she said. "I repeat. Do not look at me. Just listen."

"Hershel will be at the U.S. Consular Services Office. He'll need your help getting to Karlsruhe. Dangerous situation. Needs asylum and diplomatically protected travel arrangements. I'll be there later with an affidavit attesting to his soundness of mind." That said, Julia left without looking at Avey.

While waiting at the Consular Services Office, Avey was approached by a man who looked at him with his head inclined. "Do I know you?" the man asked.

"I don't think so," Avey responded.

"Oh, wait. From the television. You're a famous lawyer, aren't you? Sure, that's where I saw you."

The man put his hand out. "I'm Tzvi," Manolo said, "and you are?"

"Avey Maisel."

"Well. A pleasure to meet you. I'll tell my wife I shook your hand. A real pleasure," he said, as he walked out the front door.

Manolo's voice crackled out across Jerusalem, "Pay dirt. Target traveling toward American Consular Office. 14 David Flusser. Allow passage. Final ID mine. Final action mine."

After saying that, he walked slowly to the left and stood in the shadow of the serpentine cement walls of the parking garage. Here, out of Avey Meisel's sight, he rested his right hand on a revolver in his jacket pocket and waited.

At that same moment, a conference meeting between four individuals was concluding. They had gathered on a screen. Each was darkened to the point of being near featureless. The voices were distorted, except to one another. The figure in the center was larger than the other three who were spaced equidistant from each other and in a circle around the central figure. The name printed under the central figure was D'Arte. Names printed under the others were, reading clockwise from D'Arte's right, Sueton, Ovar, and Mari.

D'Arte spoke. "I've heard quite enough. Egon and Dorin would like nothing better than for us to stumble into the idiocy of crating a martyr. Agreed?" The others murmured an assent.

"And what for," D'Arte continued, "in the hope of stopping a court case in Germany? How many legions has that Court to enforce its order? Indeed, how many legions has Germany?" There was no reply.

"Issue an abort," he asserted. "Good day gentlemen, and thank you." The screen went blank.

When Avey saw Hershel crossing the street in front of the building, he rushed out to meet him. Hershel reached the sidewalk that bisected the circular driveway and froze, staring at Manolo on the sidewalk to the right of the entrance. Manolo's gun was raised beneath a face that was contorted with fury. The old man went to his knees and looked heavenward. Avey could see Hershel's lips moving in what appeared to be a final prayer.

Seeing Manolo's gun raised and pointed at Hershel's heart, Avey stopped before crossing the driveway to where Hershel waited. Avey expected the explosion that occurs when a hammer at the beginning of a barrel ignites gunpowder and sends a bullet through the barrel into a pumping heart, at a speed that defies argument and destroys a human life in seconds.

As seconds went by, however, he noticed that Manolo had stiffened slightly. Yet, the man kept his gun trained on Hershel. "What the hell is going on here?" Avey shouted at Manolo.

Manolo said nothing, but kept his gun leveled at the old man. Avey rushed forward toward Hershel. When he was directly in front of him, Avey went to his knees, putting his body between the killer and Hershel. He stared at his client's face, expecting that death would now quickly take them both.

After a moment, Avey turned to look at Manolo and was surprised to see that the gunman was putting his weapon in his jacket pocket and was walking quickly up David Flusser Street. He was soon out of sight, having turned the corner behind the parking structure.

Hershel's eyes were filled with tears as Avey helped him into the Consular building. "I was ready to go," he said.

"Shit, so was I," the lawyer said, laughing. "What the hell was that all about?"

"Long story," said Hershel.

Julia found them in the cafeteria. Hershel was talking. Avey had put his right hand on Hershel's left hand as Hershel sipped coffee.

After a time, Avey called Steiner, filling him in on what had occurred. The three of them waited for a call back from Steiner.

A half hour later, Steiner told Avey that they were expected at the U.S. Consulate on Agron Road in Jerusalem. Carla Dorin, Chief-of-Staff to the Chancellor, had obtained a commitment from the American Consul to ensure safe passage for Hershel from Jerusalem to Karlsruhe. Until the details for secure travel could be made, Hershel was to remain at the U.S. Consulate.

Julia and Avey cleared their schedules so that they could stay with Hershel until later that evening when he was to board a flight direct to Karlsruhe. He was to be flanked by American security guards the whole way.

Avey and Steiner considered reporting Manolo's crimes to the Israeli police and decided not to do so. The police might want to detain Hershel as a witness and thereby expose him to delays in getting to Karlsruhe. Delays in Israel might possibly jeopardize his security.

After Hershel was safely away, Julia and Avey returned to their usual activities. They were to await word from Steiner about the Court proceedings and whether or not they should appear as witnesses in the upcoming abstract review hearing.

The following day, Julia met with Sarah and Hershel's sons, Nathan and Levi, to tell them what had happened. The hoax of his recanting and reuniting with the family had sewn confusion. When Sarah heard the whole story, she bitterly foreclosed any possible relationship with her husband, proclaiming, "My husband is dead to me. He's turned his back on everything that makes sense. He deserves whatever will happen to him."

Julia looked at the sons, pleadingly. "You know, he's trying to find a way toward peace, real peace."

Nathan answered. "There can be no peace granted to a sheep that bleats out pleas of guilty to all who will hear him. To that sheep, there is only slaughter ahead. Ignominious, inevitable slaughter."

Chapter 25

When the eight judges in their red robes walked into the courtroom from a doorway behind the rostrum, everyone stood. The judges ceremoniously took off their hats. The clerk noted the date, April 8, 2013, and called the session to order.

Anne sat next to Hershel in the front row. Every seat in the room, including the balcony, was occupied.

Frederick Egon rose from his chair at the counsel table and addressed the Court. "My role in this portion of the abstract review, is limited as a result of the unusual position taken by the defendant, Hershel Selden. As a result, unless you rule to the contrary, we need not concern ourselves with such matters as statutes of limitation, whether crimes did or did not precede our own enactments, or whether a war crime committed in 1948 can be considered to have caused or contributed to a suicide bombing almost sixty years later. The work of the Court," Egon said, "apparently narrows down to culpability, as we have long-defined that term. Putting the concept of culpability another way, under all the circumstances, is it appropriate to hold Mr. Selden accountable, criminally, for his conduct?"

Anne had, long before the hearing, begun to read about the Constitutional Court at Karlsruhe. It was regarded as one of the most important tribunals in the world. And the concept of needing to determine culpability was a fascination for her. Guilt alone was not enough.

She recalled an interesting hypothetical example from one of the articles she'd read about culpability. An accused, in the late 1800s stole a loaf of bread. He may have been guilty of theft, but culpability for that act belonged to his employer who, without notice, closed the factories in that town without providing sustenance for employees as they tried to find work elsewhere. The discussion on culpability noted that it is less appreciated in countries which use juries for criminal cases. There, juries are informed of the statute against stealing, told of the facts concerning the theft of bread, and are directed to take nothing else into consideration before making a determination of guilt or innocence. In Germany, Anne read, judges alone hear the cases. They tend to dig far deeper into criminal matters by investigating an array of causes and circumstances. They look for true responsibility, and they call that a search for culpability.

Judge Wilfred Schoft began the inquiry by calling an array witnesses to testify. Anne knew some of their names. They were renowned historians. Each of them gave the clerk copies of papers they had published on the subject of their testimony before answering Schoft's questions related to The Puppet's Case.

Each testified briefly, but in stunning detail, about different aspects of two thousand years of anti-Semitism throughout Europe, the Middle East, and North Africa. They noted how matters worsened in the 20th century. Several professors spoke of Adolph Hitler's efforts to exterminate all Jewry. And the pogroms continued in Europe, they said, even after the Second World War was concluded. Throughout the airing of that evidence, the courtroom was as still as a crypt. Every word, every nuance of evil seemed to have been imbibed and impressed on all who were present.

Hershel listened to the testimony without moving or reacting in any way. Every mention, however, of Christian perfidy sent tremors of regret through Anne. Those acts of wrongdoing would never have been condoned by the Jesus she knew. Several times, she wanted to cry out during descriptions of hate-fueled conduct by Popes, potentates, and villagers in his name. Where and how, she grieved, had Christianity been so turned from Christ's teachings?

At the break for lunch, Anne found herself holding onto Hershel for balance. They sat in a booth in the cafeteria on the first floor with Klaus Steiner. All she could manage to eat was a cup of soup. She noticed that one of the expert witnesses, Hans Becker, was at a nearby table. She knew of his work and asked Hershel and Klaus if they wouldn't mind her talking to the man while the two of them conferred over lunch.

Becker, a thin man with slightly sunken cheeks was seated alone. He stood as Anne approached his table with her hand extended. "You are Hans Becker," she said. "I teach history myself. I'm involved in the case. I watched you testify this morning."

"Yes, I saw you seated next to Mr. Selden."

"Just wanted to tell you how moved I was by your depiction of pogroms that continued in Europe, even after World War II had ended."

"Thank you. Please have a seat. Is it alright that we speak?" he asked.

"I think so," Anne responded, "Hershel has essentially pleaded guilty. That's been a long-sought goal on his part. I don't think he has defenses that might be compromised by our talking. And, in any event, you have finished testifying." Becker nodded his approval to Anne's assertion that they could talk to one another.

"But what interests me," she said, "is how much this Court is paying attention to everything else that was going on in the world at the time."

"Aha, you're seeing the concept of culpability at work, maybe for the first time. It's confusing, and you want to know where it might lead."

"Exactly," Anne said.

"I'm interested in the same question. So are some of my colleagues," he responded.

"What do you and your colleagues hope might occur here?"

"We're wishing for a miracle."

Anne laughed. "Do you mean intervention by a divine agency."

"Close enough," Hans responded. "You have eight highly trained, conservatively oriented judges in that room. Their first reaction will be to simply rule on Selden's application and select a suitable punishment if they find him adequately culpable himself. Correct?"

"Yes," Anne said, "I assume that's what they have in mind to do."

"But," Hans took a bite of his sandwich and thoughtfully chewed before continuing. "I've had conversations with the rapporteur. He appears to see well beyond the confines of this case. What if culpability in this matter lies overwhelmingly not with Mr. Selden, but elsewhere?"

"End of case, and we go home?"

"But what if your going home turns out to be just the beginning of the matter?"

"The beginning?"

"Yes, the beginning of this Court at Karlsruhe actually taking on the serious work of dealing with the major causes of turmoil and war in this world?"

"And if they take on that bigger responsibility?" Anne asked.

"That will be the miracle."

"It's interesting that you use a religious word in this context," Anne said, waiving a hand in the air to signify that they were in a court of law and not in a cathedral.

"I use the word because I know that the servitude we are all experiencing is a bondage of greater proportions than this Earth has ever known. At the same time, the planet is hurtling toward destruction." He paused before continuing. "And the great teachings that can lead us out of it have been reduced to irrelevance by arrogance and greed."

The two of them were quiet for a moment. Anne began to think through what Becker meant by human bondage never before experienced. She had a fair understanding of what he meant when he said we were destroying the Earth by not being able shepherds. But she knew precisely what he had in mind about how little the teachings of Christ had come to mean.

Becker shifted his gaze upward, toward the ceiling where the Court had been in session. "I look to those eight red-robed judges as the very last hope."

Chapter 26

In the afternoon session, a number of eminent historians detailed the promises that were made to both Arabs and Jews by the major powers in the first fifty years of the 20th century. Both had been promised hegemony over Palestine.

Professor Arnold Ottenger, from McGill University, an expert on the British Empire, then described how the British had been in charge of Palestine at the end of the Second World War. "Impoverished and dispirited by the war, they simply pulled out, leaving Arabs and Jews to face one another in a world without rational constraints of any sort."

Professor Peter Naessens from the University of Southern Denmark took the stand. Portly and muscular, with a deep baritone voice, he picked up where Ottenger left off. "After the Second World War," he said, "the hopes of humanity for peace and world order were dashed yet again. This world was left without rational constraints of any sort, just as Professor Ottenger testified."

Looking at Hershel Selden, Naessens continued. "Your defendant in this case found himself in a world that had been denied humanitarian governance. He was hounded, orphaned by the nation-states, forced into being an intruder, and plunged into war, all with no hope whatsoever of help from any organized authority in the world. I'm sure he would have abided by orders from such a power. But there was none. He found himself in that most primitive of situations, kill or be killed."

"Surely," asked Judge Schoft, "you don't mean to say the United Nations was of no assistance in that regard?"

"I do," the witness shouted back. "Without an independent source of revenue, the United Nations was powerless. It could not muster forces. Indeed, any member of the Security Council could stop any action it wished to undertake at any time. In short, the United Nations was a thoroughly impotent organization."

Naessens leaned forward in his chair. "Far worse. It gave the impression that there was world governance when, in fact, there was none."

"Some people say," said Schoft, "that there has been no World War III because of the existence of the United Nations."

"That's rubbish, plain and simple," replied Naessens.

"Kindly explain that conclusion, if you will."

"I'll do better," the witness said. "I refer you to two maps on pages 82 and 83 of the paper that I've provided for this Court."

Schoft, the other judges, and all counsel at the table reached for the professor's report. The witness waited before continuing. "Page 82 is a map showing all countries of the world in the autumn of 1945. Page 83 is the same map with red smudges everywhere there have been and everywhere there are, at present, armed conflicts. You will notice that while there has not been a so-called World War III since 1945, we have been and we are, in fact, experiencing a World At War."

Naessens held up his copy. "Continuous," he said. "Nonstop." Page 83 was nearly all smudged red. Huge swatches of Africa, Asia, South America, Central America, and the Middle East were blood red. "Does it matter to the grieving widow or to an orphan," he thundered, "that their loved ones died in a World War or in a World at War?"

"Thank you Professor Naessens."

As the witness was about to rise from his chair, he stopped, sat back down, and stared at the judges. "Look," he said to them, "I have three children. I send them to sleep every night, knowing that their world is in complete chaos. If you don't weigh in and bring about a true world order, you will be condemning my children and yours to live on an endangered Earth, ruled by those who seek only profits and who have neither conscience nor pity." He paused. "It's up to you."

One of the judges called for a recess. Anne leaned toward Hershel and whispered, "I was thinking of Kevin and Amy."

"So was I," he said, reaching for her hand.

The next witness when the Court reconvened was Professor Avrom Barsky from the University of Pennsylvania. Tall, thin, and bent slightly forward by age, he seated himself with the slow precision practiced by those who have come to know frailty.

Anne was intrigued by the sight of him here in Karlsruhe. Recognized as a significant intellectual in most of the world, Barsky had been shunned by the media in the United States. And he was largely disregarded, as well, by American academics. He was one of those people, Anne reflected, whose words and thoughts would be allowed to surface only as part of one-day-stellar-coverage in lengthy obituaries.

"At this point in the hearing," Judge Wilfred Schoft said to the witness, Avrom Barsky, "we are struggling to understand whether there is, in fact, governance in our world."

"Yes," Barsky said, "there's governance, but not the sort that works for the general welfare. We never came close to that."

Barsky went on to describe world dominance by the United States as being merely the latest in a long line of empires. It differs, he said, from preceding ones, like the Dutch, the British, and the French, by the manner in which the American Empire is being run. Older ones operated openly, he told the judges, mostly using military forces to control populations and administrators to govern. "On the other hand, Americans operate through the use of stealth," he told them.

"In a manner reminiscent of Shakespeare's Iago," he testified, "the United States has used and uses underhanded and fraudulent tactics to undermine independent foreign leaders. In this manner, dictators have been installed who accept policies friendly to American business interests."

Most of the next day was taken up with hearing Barsky disclose, in detail, such matters as the installation of a military dictatorship in Greece after the Second World War rather than to allow the election of communists and socialists to leadership positions. He testified to American complicity in the murder of Patrice Lumumba, the first elected prime minister of the Congo. He took the Judges through a thorough description of how the United States the engineered the take-down of Iran's democratically elected, secular prime minister, Muhammad Mossadegh in 1953.

"Each destructive, criminal action, and I've listed hundreds of them for you in the documents that I've submitted to you," he said, "bore consequences that are with us right up to this very moment. They tore to shreds whatever hope there had been for people around the world to form positive alliances and fulfill needs of the people. Indeed, the most serious consequence of the criminal behavior of the American Empire is that people living today cannot even conceive of the possibility of governance of the people, by the people, and for the people—-to borrow a phrase by President Lincoln. As I said earlier, we never even got close to that."

"What do you suggest be done?" asked Judge Schoft.

"That's not a hard question," Barsky said in a quiet monotone. "Do right now what should have been done in 1945. All else leads to mischief."

"Mischief?" asked Schoft, smiling.

"There's no other term to describe the farce of a world body that was never allowed to function, yet gives the impression that it is all that can be expected," replied Barsky.

There was a brief silence. Barsky continued. "Mr. Selden's case is instructive. The United States, the sole power left standing in 1945, gave up no authority whatsoever to the United Nations, allowed the British to abandon Palestine, and recognized the State of Israel, but never even considered moving troops in to keep the peace. So, your Mr. Selden was left quite on his own."

"You know," he continued, "there are billions of people like Mr. Selden in this Iago-constructed world. They are trapped in failed and failing states, sites of civil war and unrest, mass migrations, and places where starvation threatens whole regions. Thievery and murder become the norm when there is no hope and no effective governance. I suggest you do something about that."

"Professor Barsky," Judge Schoft asked, "would you kindly clarify what you mean when you say that we——this Constitutional Court in Karlsruhe, Germany——should do something about that?"

The witness was silent for a moment. Then he asked, "Is there not a provision in the law dealing with the concept of impossibility?"

"Of course," said Schoft.

"As I understand it," Barsky said, "when an obligation is impossible to perform..."

"The law," Schoft continued, "excuses performance regarding that obligation. But what has that to do with the failure of governance?"

"Members of the Security Council of the United Nations—-let's just take the United States—-can exert, by use of the veto, total control of that world body. Total control," Barsky said slowly.

"So," he continued, "there is, in fact, no world body. It can be and so often was simply shut down by one veto or the threat of one veto that it doesn't exist as a world body. It's a phantom, and clinging to its chimera as though that body holds out any hope of true governance is foolhardy and impossible. Legally impossible, as well as morally bankrupt. That's your law of impossibility."

"So, this Court," Judge Schoft began..."

"Has to see through the fog of deception so that a new international body can be created."

There was stillness in the Court. Judge Schoft rose from his chair and walked toward the witness. "Isn't it incumbent," he said, "upon the American people to rectify this problem? More appropriately, shouldn't they be directing their representatives to the United Nations to act in a manner consistent with principles of world justice?"

Before Barsky could respond, Schoft added, "Shouldn't the American people be weighing in on restricting improper use of the American veto power at the United Nations?"

Barsky's demeanor turned sad. He said, "The American public has little understanding of such things and knows almost nothing about foreign policy carried out in their name. A nation of the misinformed, they were driven to make war, brutally and senselessly all around the world, against a political philosophy——communism——beginning in 1945, while the United Nations just stood by. Count the dead."

The witness shook his head, as though in disbelief. "And most recently, they were driven to make war, again brutally and senselessly all around the world, against a tactic of resistance, the use of terror. And by making war against that tactic——terrorism——they expand the resistance, creating new wars, wars without an end in sight, while the United Nations just stands by. Count the dead."

"Who makes that happen?" asked Judge Schoft, standing within feet of Professor Barsky.

"Profiteers who have captured the government and control the media," said Barsky. "And matters will grow continuously worse. International corporations are now conducting a mad scramble for resources around the world, while this planet is fast becoming uninhabitable. Wars, resistance, famine, and mass migrations, will only proliferate as the affects of global climate changes become more and more manifest."

The witness paused. "The American people have been rendered powerless. The world still awaits governance of the people, by the people, and for the people before it's too late."

"Thank you," Judge Schoft said.

Professor Barsky started to get up, but was having difficulty. Judge Schoft held on to the witness' elbow, and Barsky was able to stand. Barsky, now beyond the range of the microphone that carried his voice throughout the Court, began talking softly to Judge Schoft.

Schoft listened briefly, picked up the microphone, put it in front of the witness who was now standing a few steps from where he had been seated. Schoft asked the Professor, "Would you kindly repeat for this Court what you just told me?"

"Culpability is an interesting concept," said Barsky, "in light of these proceedings." Looking at the Judges, "If you do not accept your responsibility to reconfigure world governance along the lines of what's being discussed here, then you are culpable and responsible for the worldwide conflagration that has already begun."

"You've said," Judge Schoft asked, "that this Court needs to look into doing what should have been done in 1945. What exactly do you consider it appropriate for our Court to do at this juncture?"

Professor Barsky turned around. With help, he sat back down in the chair and leaned toward the judges. Speaking slowly, he said, "If I were you, I would hold that it is impossible, legally impossible, to expect the United Nations to function in such a way as to assure peace and survival."

He looked at them, as if to see whether there might be questions. Seeing no hands raised, as if in a classroom, he continued. "It being impossible for that body, controlled as it is by vast economic interests, you must determine that it is now appropriate for your country to no longer be bound to membership in the United Nations."

"And then?" asked Judge Schoft.

"As I suggested, begin anew. Do now what should have been done in 1945. That's your responsibility under the law and to the world."

Chapter 27

The following morning, Attorney General Egon called Hershel Selden to the stand. By agreement between Egon, Steiner, and Judge Schoft, Hershel and the witnesses to follow would be questioned by the Attorney General.

Egon began by asking Hershel where he was on January 4, 2013. Hershel said he was staying at a hotel in New Brunswick, New Jersey, in the United States. Egon then took Hershel through his encounter with the man who said his name might be Garrett Williams. Testimony included Williams' statement that he was with an organization that directed world affairs. Hershel testified that Williams ordered him to recant his statements to the Court and ask that his matter be withdrawn. If Hershel went along with that, according to Williams, he would be taken care of for the rest of his life. If he refused, Williams said he'd be a dead man in forty-eight hours.

"Did Mr. Williams tell you why his organization wanted you to abandon the proceedings in Karlsruhe?"

"He did."

"What reason did he give you?"

"Williams said that this case threatens the foundations of what they had put together over the last hundred years."

"Did you know what he meant?"

"No, but I asked Anne Whalen. She said..."

"Ms. Whalen is in court," Egon said to the Judges. "We'll have her testify directly."

Turning back to Hershel, Egon asked, "Did Williams, during that conversation, make mention of Anne Whalen?"

"Yes. He knew that we had a close relationship. It was clear that his group had been spying on us."

"How did you know that?"

"Williams quoted, verbatim, from private conversations that we had. One was a phone call I made to Anne from Karlsruhe. The other was at the airport in the United States when she picked me up. Mr. Egon, at the airport, she and I were practically whispering to one another."

"What did you conclude from the fact that these very private conversations between you and Anne had been intruded upon?"

"I was forced to believe that, unless I took special pains to evade them, every communication everywhere I went would be heard and recorded."

"What, if anything, did you do thereafter concerning the need for secrecy?"

"I met with Anne the same day, alone and in a very cloistered place, after taking pains to make sure we had not been followed. And I met with my nephew, Alan Selden, on January 8, at his office, after taking similar precautions. The burdens imposed by eavesdropping," Hershel began to say and then stopped himself.

"Please finish your statement," Egon urged.

"It's pure fear. You're afraid for the safety of people you most need to talk with. So you feel isolation. And you begin to look at yourself differently. Suddenly you're like an animal that's being hunted."

"Why did you meet with your nephew?"

"To tell him that if I disappeared or was found dead, he was to look into the circumstances. I was not about to take my own life, and I was not going to abandon my application before this Court."

The questioning that followed took Hershel through his kidnapping off the streets of New Brunswick to his extraordinary rendition to Israel where newspaper accounts had already told of his recanting of testimony and his assertion that he'd not been of sound mind. Hershel described Manolo, the escape, and his connecting with both his psychologist, Julia Pozar, and his lawyer, Avey

Maisel. He ended his testimony with a description of Manolo aiming a gun at him as he went to his knees in front of the U.S. Consular Services Office in Jerusalem.

Egon called Alan Selden to testify about his conversation with Hershel and Alan's viewing of the video tape of an imposter dressed to look like Hershel who was traveling on Hershel's passport to Israel. Julia Pozar testified about hiding Hershel overnight and putting Avey Maisel in touch with him at the Consular Services Office. Then Avey testified about talking to Manolo just before Manolo was about to kill Hershel on the street outside that office.

"Are you certain that the man who spoke to you in the Consular Services Office was the same man who held the gun up to shoot Hershel Selden?"

"Absolutely positive. It was the same man."

"And you put yourself between that man and Selden. Why did you do that?"

"I'm not sure," Maisel said. "It was foolish. Certainly. At the same time, I know that justice had gone awry in Israel, and that somehow what Hershel was doing might help set things straight. So, I felt the need to protect him."

"What do you mean when you say that Selden's case might help to set things straight?"

Avey thought for a moment. "Israel," he said, "is like a soup with two ingredients: fear and hate. It has cooked for so long that it's become a sludge from which there is no escape. Hershel brings understanding. They tried to silence him, saying he was mentally unfit. That was ludicrous. I believe he brings understanding in such measure that with his way of thinking, the sludge of fear and hate can be washed away, and Israel can become a place of peace and brotherhood."

After Avey, Anne was called to testify. "What did you conclude about Garrett Williams," Egon asked, "when Hershel Selden first told you of their conversation?"

"My first impression of Williams was that he did, in fact, represent a powerful organization."

"Why?"

"Because his behavior was audacious, and he asked nothing for himself."

"Was your first impression confirmed?"

"Yes. Spying in this modern age of electronics requires an organization, one that functions within serious networks that presently intrude into private lives around the world. And certainly, Mr. Egon, what that group did to Hershel after the first encounter is all the confirmation one needs. They are powerful, and they are ruthless."

"What's your opinion," Egon asked, "about Williams' claim that they controlled world affairs for the last hundred years?"

"The evidence for that is clear, and one does not have to be a first tier historian to see it."

"Kindly explain."

"A hundred years ago, Americans wanted to take no part in the First World War in Europe. But they were duped by an amazingly effective propaganda campaign against Germany."

"What was the purpose behind pushing American entry into World War I?"

"It appears that American banks had loaned heavily to countries that had opposed Germany. Defeating Germany assured repayment. Some people called it a rich man's war and a poor man's fight."

"How could those American interests have gotten away with such an audacious action?"

"Easily," Anne responded. "All dissent was shut down, deemed un-American, and even criminalized. The effort was so successful that to this very day Americans don't have the necessary vocabulary to participate effectively in conversations that question the assumptions behind corporate control."

"What, if anything, was done back then after the World War I about international order?" asked Egon.

"The people of the world dreamed of creating international order. That dream became the League of Nations. The dream was subverted by American business interests. And the dream eludes us to this day as a result of having a United Nations that was never allowed to fully function."

"What else occurred after the First World War that has ramifications for our time?"

"There was a covert war in Russia at that time. No one speaks about it. The United States led a coalition of nations that intervened in the Russian Civil War.

It was an effort was to strangle the new communist government in its cradle. Covert wars continue as we speak. No one is allowed to try different paths to a better future."

Anne shook her head and added, "The Cold War was an abomination during which Americans sought to punish all who had a different political philosophy. As Professor Barsky said, count the dead, and there was no international organization that one could go to in order to stop the carnage."

Looking at Avey Maisel, she added, "And the present war against terrorism has been so successful for corporate interests that it's turning the whole world into a soup of sludge so thick with fear and hate, as Mr. Maisel put it, that there is little likelihood of bringing about true international order. The world is presently bogged down in fraudulently induced propaganda. There exists no means to bring about justice."

After Anne's testimony, Frederick Egon stood and turned to the Judges. "I have submitted troubling affidavits to you about how my efforts to obtain evidence are being rebuffed. Even though the man who called himself Garrett Williams traversed public places, I am being told that no camera footage of him exists. All images of the man who traveled on Mr. Selden's passport have disappeared, and I've even been told that no camera footage exists of the infamous Manolo, even though he walked in and out of the American Consular Services Office in Jerusalem."

Egon walked to the center of the Judge's bench. "The fact that these crucial bits of information have been made unavailable is further confirmation that this organization exists and exerts significant influence in world affairs."

The Attorney General then asked for a moment. He went to the front row and briefly conferred with a man and a woman who Hershel told Anne were representatives of the German legislature. He turned to address the Judges again. "It's time that we begin to ponder the most serious of questions: Are they not making puppets of us all?"

Anne squeezed Hershel's hand and looked at him. A tear had made its way down his face.

Chapter 28

On the following morning, a day that promised clouds and light rain, the proceedings began with Wilfred Schoft making statements to his fellow Judges. Anne thought of them more as the musings of a thoroughly educated man allowing himself the luxury of intuitive explorations.

"During yesterday's session," he began, "the Attorney General asked us to focus on the existence of a group that drives this world in destructive ways for its own benefit. And Mr. Egon concluded that we should consider whether or not that group is making puppets of us all."

Judge Schoft folded his hands. "My career," he continued, "is likely to stretch out thirty more years to retirement. During that time, it's likely that I will be judging a long line of cases where individuals will have been driven to commit unspeakable acts. But isn't it incumbent upon us now to deal with those people who create the stages upon which endless scenes of violence are played out?"

The judge paused. Anne could not come close to guessing what he might say next. "Those who subverted the League of Nations set the stage for violence and are now long gone. Similarly, those who falsely claimed that the Soviet Union intended in 1945 to conquer the world by force brought warfare to four continents, and they too, having created a World at War, are gone.

"Meanwhile, we judges in Germany and judges around the world overlook those who subvert the peace, as though it is their right to do so.

"Well, I wish to cast a wider net and concentrate on those who, at present, are setting the stages for harm and are making a mockery of justice. Their methods can be as subtle as a well-placed defamation or a seismic event created to bring disorder to large areas of the world. With all that in mind, I call Dr. Jacob Frieder to the stand."

While the witness was approaching his seat, Presiding Judge Fritz Leber addressed his fellow judges and the audience. "Judge Schoft is about to elicit testimony from a series of witnesses. He has shared with me what they will say. I am convinced that their testimony is germane to our undertaking in this matter."

Steiner leaned back, away from the counsel table, and whispered to Hershel, "Most unusual. I have no idea..."

Dr. Frieder, of the University of Zurich, sat in the witness chair. Tall, with sensitive features and dark eyes, he began his testimony by listing his degrees in physics and chemistry. He went on to tell of the books and articles he'd written over the past thirty years. The list seemed endless to Anne. Judge Schoft was in no hurry. With credentials thus made rather solid, the questioning began.

"Dr. Frieder," Judge Schoft asked, "it appears that you have written extensively concerning the events of September 11, 2001 in the United States."

"Correct," Frieder responded.

"Why have you focused on those events?"

Frieder moved back in his chair and looked toward the ceiling. "Because I like to sleep at night."

Judge Schoft laughed, "Doctor, how did we get, with such suddenness, to your nighttime difficulties?"

"Some years ago, I had trouble sleeping because it was clear to me that the events of 9/11 were staged, and most people have been fooled. They seem not to be able to think critically about those events."

"Doctor, you've said and I quote, the events of 9/11 are many orders of magnitude worse than the Reichstag fire, unquote. What did you mean by that?"

"The Reichstag fire gave a cabal known as the Nazi party political control over Germany. The events of 9/11 have given a cabal in the United States the self declared right to make war whenever and wherever it wishes throughout the world."

"Dr. Frieder, within the purview of your specialty, what proof, if any, can you bring to this court concerning the veracity of claims made that the United States was attacked by Arab terrorists on September 11, 2001?"

"Let's begin," he said, "with the false claim that the Pentagon was struck by an airplane." Frieder then described, in detail, the length and structure of the wings of a Boeing 747. He held up a photograph of that portion of the Pentagon that was taken within moments of impact. "There is no debris from wings and struts and engines whatsoever on the ground. That is impossible," he shouted, "impossible for an airliner to have hit a steel reinforced concrete building without leaving an extensive field of debris."

Anne had a sinking feeling as she watched Frieder testify. How many opportunities did she miss in her classes to allow inquiry into those facts? She recalled the occasional student who tried and was shouted down by others as being a conspiracy nut. Why had she been so intimidated that the matter was not even discussed in her classes?

Frieder then went on to describe World Trade Center Building #7. Again, he used the term impossible to describe how a building 610 feet tall, consisting of 47 stories that took up an entire city block could come crashing down in a perfect seven second free fall. It had not been struck by aircraft. It came down some seven hours after the destruction of the nearby twin towers. "Never, in all the history of mankind upon this planet has such a total, perfect destruction been brought about other than when accomplished by a purposefully controlled demolition."

The witness then described the collapses of the twin towers. "Again, only controlled demolitions," he said, "could have brought them down in a nine second free fall, perfectly within their own footprint."

"What are the odds," Judge Schoft asked, "of those three buildings, World Trade Center Buildings 1, 2, and 7, coming down in free fall, exactly into the area of their bases without there having been controlled demolitions?"

Frieder smiled as though he'd been waiting years for that question to be asked. "All three?" he said. "Odds? There are not enough zeros in the universe to express the lack of possibility for such events to have taken place on one day in one place. Not enough zeros! By that I mean not one chance in a million or a billion or a trillion or more. No, your honor, there are simply not enough zeros to express just how impossible it is to accept the official version of those events. It was not Arab terrorists acting independently aboard airplanes who brought those buildings down."

The witness concluded by saying that he felt honor bound to speak the truth. He thanked Judge Schoft for allowing him that opportunity.

The next witness called was Col. Dieter Kestrick, a retired NATO and German Air Force officer. His thinning hair was now all grey. Slightly built, with soft features and what looked like a permanent smile, he reached for his eyeglass case while making himself comfortable. The glasses he put on were small, steel framed bifocals.

After going through the witness' extensive military experience, Judge Schoft asked, "Colonel Kestrick, you're on record as having said that the official story of the September 11 attack is absurd. Kindly elaborate."

Kestrick then testified about American military procedures that had been in place for decades. If and when airliners were to go off-course, jets would be scrambled within minutes to intercept and shoot them down, if necessary. In two hours that morning on September 11, not one fighter jet was scrambled to investigate multiple threats. "That could only have been the result of an order to stand down," he said.

He then described the complex high speed maneuvering required for large airliners to hit the twin towers in New York City. "Those maneuvers could hardly have been done by experienced pilots. And I say they were impossible, absolutely impossible to accomplish, by terrorists acting alone with only modest training."

"And the strike against the Pentagon," he continued. "No one, myself included, could possibly have brought an airliner to hit that structure within feet of ground level. No one! The Pentagon, quite obviously, had been hit by a guided missile."

The witness leaned back, took off his glasses and looked at the judges. "The probability is that the two airliners which struck the twin towers were also guided that morning from the ground. My guess is that Building #7 was the guidance center. For that reason, it was destroyed by a series of controlled demolition explosions later that day."

At the conclusion of Kestrick's testimony, Judge Schoft turned to his fellow Judges. "That's just a small portion of the proofs concerning 9/11. As a result of those staged events, how many puppets in how many places took how many lives believing all the while that they were doing what was needed to be done? And of all those newly created warriors, how many might we find culpable when the guilty escape even criticism by a cowed world community? Finally, I ask, when will it all end if we don't make efforts to terminate this ongoing charade?"

Chapter 29

They gathered for dinner in a modest restaurant at the Renaissance Karlsruhe Hotel where Anne, Hershel, Avey, Julia, and Alan were staying. Klaus Steiner was the last to arrive and was shown to their round table set for six near the windows that looked out onto Ruppurrer Street.

Klaus sat to Anne's left, next to Alan. To her right were Avey and Julia. Hershel was across from Anne, with his back to the floor-to-ceiling windows. She thought to say that Hershel ought not sit there and then realized that perhaps this whole group needed to be in some far corner of the room so that they might be kept from harm. At the end of that train of thought, however, Anne decided to say nothing about security. She'd been thinking a good deal about her fears and about her desires for security. Hadn't fears and desires for security been the cause of all of this turmoil?

Klaus and Alan were talking to each other about how incredible it was that Judge Schoft had called upon Jacob Frieder and Dieter Kestrick to testify about the 9/11 attacks. To punctuate their conversation, Klaus raised his glass. "A toast," he said, "to a man of courage, to Wilfred Schoft."

"And let's not leave out Judge Leber," added Alan.

"I second toasts to them both," said Julia, who had been talking to Avey about his protecting Hershel at the Consular Office. "Some guys," she laughed, "just have the biggest," she paused, "senses of obligation."

As Anne raised her glass and laughed along with the others, she recalled the salient facts that Frieder and Kestrick had brought out in court. What they said was so obvious. It was as if those men found it necessary to remind the world that the law of gravity had not been repealed. Impossible was the word that kept echoing through her consciousness. Three buildings, same day, fall precisely in their own footprint. Impossible. An airplane hits a steel reinforced concrete building and disappears. Disappears. She mouthed the word impossible, and it roared inside her mind.

Anne took a sip of wine with the others while thinking about how she had failed to stand up for the truths that Frieder and Kestrick had stated. She recalled how subtle she'd been as she discouraged one particular student in her class, a young man who tried to bring up a few of those facts. Instead of responding herself, Anne looked about the class, waiting for another student to comment. The response she sought came quickly enough from another student. "That's a bunch of conspiracy crap. Whyancha cut it out? Huh? Whancha just cut it out?"

There were so many ways of dealing honorably with the student who was wrestling on his own with 9/11 falsehoods. She chose so badly, so cowardly. His questions had called for a teachable moment in so many ways, and she'd brought shame upon herself. Why was it necessary for a judge in another country to be risking his life and his career to bring forward facts and conclusions that she should have been pursuing and teaching about year in and year out? Why couldn't she have been true to the obligations imposed upon her as a teacher?

Conversations at the table, for Anne, turned to a blur of incoherent sounds as she struggled with ghosts in hosts of classrooms filled with young people who had long ago graduated but were never adequately educated. "I knew those things," she said quietly.

"What?" asked Avey who was sitting to her right. Others at the table stopped talking.

"What Frieder and Kestrick said. Some students talked about it. Once in a while, a teacher would mention it and quickly say 'but don't quote me.'" Anne, with her hands clasped in her lap, slowly rocked back and forth. "I said nothing. So many years went by."

Avey reached out and held her hand. "Look," he said, "you can't blame yourself, not for a minute, because..."

"So what does that make me?" she interrupted, "a fraud? Maybe a whore?"

"Anne," Hershel pleaded, "you're nothing of the kind."

"No?" she responded, "So why did I keep silent? Nothing was to jeopardize my teacher's pension or pit me against the loudmouths who blathered the propaganda. I can't remember. I may have even thought about the companies that give grants to my University. God, what did all that have to do with the noble profession of teaching?"

"One time," she said. "I even let a loudmouth student shout down a kid who'd been trying to come to grips with the truths that Frieder and Kestrick talked about."

"I know what you're saying," said Julia. "There's something hypnotic about going along. We all do it, almost all the time. The benefits are instantaneous. Please don't be too hard on yourself."

Anne wished she could be talking to Julia alone. There was so much more to say. Hadn't she sinned in preferring comfort to duty? "You know that I think in terms of sinning?"

"Of course," Julia replied.

There was a long silence at the table. Anne struggled to put her thoughts into words. Julia waited with a smile. "We'll all know soon," Anne said, pausing, "but my sense is that God is about love and justice and mercy."

"That's beautiful," said Julia.

"So, when we're not about love and justice and mercy, and we look the other way, of what benefit is confession and being forgiven?"

"A comfort, perhaps," Julia replied.

"And the comforts received multiply while the map of the world swims in blood, and my looking away has helped to make it possible for us all to be living in a World at War, dominated by lies."

"I think we're all in the place you're describing," said Hershel. "For me, it took the deaths of Adele and the family. Until that tragedy, I believed all the trash they served up to us."

"Like Arabs deserved no better," said Avey. "That one had been burned into my brain. I let that lie live for too long into my life."

"In my neighborhood," said Steiner, "growing up, we were told what a shame it was that Hitler had not been permitted to complete his solution to the Jewish problem, and I believed that too."

"Until?" asked Julia.

"The German government, itself, started saying that it had all been a lie. Before that, I and millions of my countrymen swore that Jews were the devils. Killing them made perfect sense."

Julia turned to Anne, "So where the hell was true independence of thought allowed? Who among us was anywhere near love and justice and mercy for all. That thinking might have existed somewhere in dreams, but not here on Earth where we were all being mired down in lies."

"How did we get so far," Anne asked, "from the ideal that God calls for?"

Julia considered the question. "One very thoughtful researcher," she said, "a man by the name of Julian Jaynes, from Princeton, produced evidence that at one time, the Divine spoke to us directly. The messages we received back then were all based on love and appreciation. Then, Jaynes said, we were put on our own, to use our free will. But I think that the habit of listening for the master's message is still deeply grooved within us."

"And the message givers of today?" Anne asked.

"They use those old grooves to shove propaganda in past our fledgling powers of free will. Waves of fear and hate flood in unabated. Getting to the great truths is full time hard labor after being inundated to the core with lies."

"God," said Anne, "the cruelty goes on and..." Her voice trailed off. There was silence at the table.

"So, out of the ashes," said Steiner, "and I do mean ashes. How else does one describe Germany? Out of the ashes comes this Constitutional Court and Judges Schoft and Leber." He raised his glass again. "I have never been prouder of being a lawyer than I am now. I have never been prouder of a client than I am of Hershel Selden. And I'm honored beyond words to be in the company of his incredible friends and family. To you all, and to a better future."

Chapter 30

When the Court convened the next morning, Presiding Judge Fritz Leber, a square-jawed elderly gentleman with a craggy face highlighted by large white eyebrows, spoke. He smiled when he said, "This has been, to say the least, a most unusual hearing." He ran his right hand through a thicket of white hair. "Unless there's objection, I'm about to rule that the testimony portion of this matter is closed." Judge Leber waited. Hearing no objection, he ruled that the testimony portion of the case was closed.

Looking at Hershel, Leber squinted slightly, as though he were studying a different type of human. "At it's core, this matter involves a determination of whether or not Mr. Selden is to be held responsible for distant consequences of a war crime he committed near Jerusalem in the year 1948."

He paused, folded his hands, and addressed the audience. "This case has brought visitors to the Court from other jurisdictions. Many of you may not be familiar with German jurisprudence. Please allow me to make a few observations. We, unlike many other nations, do not use juries in criminal cases. Our method has been to require that judges determine the guilt or innocence of a person accused of a crime.

"So, our judges, over many generations have become unusually adept at assessing behavior that's alleged to be criminal. Of singular importance in determining guilt or innocence is the concept of culpability. What does that word mean? Briefly, it means a study of the circumstances in which the accused found himself.

"Respectfully, in countries that use juries for criminal matters, great care is taken to focus almost exclusively on the crime alleged and the wording of particular criminal statutes that the prosecutor says were violated. Using the analogy of optical lenses, countries that have juries put criminal cases under a microscope. In our jurisprudence, we look into criminal matters by using a wide-angle lens.

"Taking great pains to understand all of the circumstances surrounding a charge of criminality, we might sift through mountains of information for grains of truth upon which justice might depend. That kind of task, we feel, is for judges alone, not juries. In the end, we try our best to make determinations that get as close as possible to the truth."

Looking again at Hershel Selden, the Judge said, "This is a complex case of a man who participated in the murder of a defenseless Arab family in 1948. To this day, he has not sought to be punished for that act. He's only here to plead guilty to the murders of his own family by a young Arab suicide bomber some sixty years later. So, after all that time, Mr. Selden is saying that his crime had consequences for which he finally feels responsible."

Judge Leber looked at Klaus Steiner. "Did I get that right, counselor?" he asked.

Steiner rose. "Yes, your honor. I've struggled with the complexity of this case."

"As have we," said Judge Leber. "The only way to make sense of this series of tragedies is to subject the matter, The Puppet's Case, to the wide angle lens approach of determining culpability or true responsibility for what occurred."

The Judge then turned his attention to the audience. "And if you are visiting from other nations, you will have noted that Judge Schoft called witnesses of his own. That's because our system is not merely adversarial, where cases are brought by and are all about the litigants alone. No, our judges, on occasion, delve into matters themselves, if they deem it appropriate. That's all part of efforts we make to get to the bottom of things.

"Now, determining culpability in this case has required that we focus on the historical events surrounding the Israel/Palestine conflict. And because history has played such a large role in those events, I gave Judge Schoft, our rapporteur, great leeway in bringing out all the details that he thought appropriate."

Smiling, the Judge said, "You cannot have helped notice that Judge Schoft went far beyond the matter of the Israel/Palestine conflict." There was restrained laughter in the audience. "Judge Schoft spared no one." More laughter. "He had much to say about the United States, the United Nations, and a cabal of people who intimidate witnesses, spy on the world, and even, as he asserts, brought down the World Trade Center towers in an effort to influence a foreign policy bent on empire.

"Well, in addition to culpability and the role of judges as rapporteurs, there's another concept in German law that I must describe for those of you who may have traveled far to get here. Our judiciary exercises an important role in making sure that the laws of Germany do, in fact, support the good and welfare of our nation and its citizens. While we cannot dictate changes in laws and policies, our opinion concerning what must be done for the good and welfare of us all must be taken seriously."

The Judge arranged papers in front of him and paused while looking at them. "This case underscores a number of truths that must be faced. We now reside in a world wherein privacy is no longer respected, the dominant endeavor in international affairs appears to be plunder, murder is all too commonplace, and there is no international order that might bring about justice on a scale that's presently necessary. If that is the current state of affairs," he paused briefly to look out the windows, "then the good and welfare of our nation and its residents require that the German legislature be prepared to take bold actions to protect us."

There was a hush as Judge Leber looked down at a book in front of him. "The rights granted to us by the Constitution of Germany include human dignity, freedom, peace, and justice, but we are not an island." He looked up, "Those inviolable rights are in jeopardy if we, the German judiciary and the German legislature, fail to find a way to end the disorder that currently plagues the affairs of this Earth and threatens our citizens."

The Judge looked out toward the great windows for a few seconds before saying, almost as if he were thinking out loud, "The canvas of this world appears to be turning dark. Wherein lies the culpability? Are we free to avoid responsibility for the public good when it has been our charge, all along, to safeguard the basic rights of man, as reflected in the German Constitution?"

Shifting gears, Judge Leber said, "Getting on to procedure, I believe that all the evidence brought out in this case is germane to our inquiry. Fairness, however, requires that the testimony of all witnesses to this point be published on our website and sent to every member nation of the United Nations. In addition, the testimony will be sent to groups of people within those nations who do not believe they are well served by the nation states in which they are presently located. Responses thereto shall be permitted for the next four months. And they too will be published on our website. At that time, this hearing shall be deemed closed. As soon as possible thereafter, we will be ready to render our decision in the matter.

"One aspect of this case is most troubling. Violence has been used as a tactic of intimidation. This court wishes to receive notice of every incident where violence is used or threatened in order to influence the outcome of our decision. We require that the State of Germany use all resources necessary to protect this inquiry.

"Eavesdropping is troublesome, as well. It has been perfected to the point that none of us, not the justices, the litigants, not the representatives of the Chancellor's office, nor those of the Bundestag and the Bundesrat are being allowed privacy in communications."

Leber paused. He briefly glanced skyward before continuing. "Privacy is a sacred right. Human development depends upon it. None of us was born with perfect knowledge. We therefore require private spaces to express our thoughts, to hear an array of contrary concepts, and to change our minds when and if necessary. Proper governance cannot occur without that freedom.

"With that in mind, this Court invites all persons involved in the massive capturing and storing of communications anywhere in the world to come forward and give information about those destructive activities."

Looking at representatives of the Chancellor's office, Leber continued. "I am directing that any applicants for asylum following disclosures of violations of privacy be granted the right to hearings on asylum before this Court on the basis that no citizen can possibly enjoy human dignity and the liberties granted in Articles 1 and 2 of our Constitution while eavesdropping anywhere is allowed to continue without rigorous constraints.

"Finally, I take issue with my learned colleague, Judge Schoft, on one item. He has proposed to us that the Court may proceed to make findings on all of what he deems engines of destruction and creators of culpability. He would free us from having to deal exclusively with cases arising from determining the rights of litigants. I suggest that we stay within the parameters of our duties by calling for an array of litigants to come forward.

"Therefore, anyone who, like the plaintiff herein, feels he has been pressed unfairly into a war may apply to be a litigant in this matter. If you believe you have been forced through some engine of destruction into a condition of being stateless, you may apply to be a litigant. If you are among the many millions of people who have been forced from your homes or exiled by war and civil unrest, you are encouraged to be a litigant herein. And if you believe that the current state of world governance is insufficient to provide for the health, safety, and welfare of yourselves and your families, you are encouraged to be a litigant in this case.

"Are there any objections to the arrangements I've outlined?" Judge Leber looked about and waited. Anne noticed that there was not a sound in the room. She, herself, had stopped breathing and imagined that others were entranced as well.

"This matter is adjourned," he announced, ever so lightly striking the small round wooden disk with his gavel. The pure wood-upon-wood sound touched a responsive yearning within Anne's soul. It marked the beginning, she hoped, of a world centered upon purity, a world that would be shaped by the truths that her God had in mind for us all.

Chapter 31

Alan went to Karlsruhe with Hershel for the Court's decision. He called Anne at 10:03 a.m., her time, on October 23, 2013, excitedly saying, "I never imagined." He told her that Judge Leber made a short statement that she'll find on the first page. "The opinion is too long for them to have read from the bench. They're posting it as we speak. I'm holding a bound copy. It's unbelievable. You have to read it for yourself."

Anne ran to her office and rushed to download and copy the document. It would be 362 pages long, filled with compendious references to cases and scholarly treatises. She took the first several pages off the printer as it methodically read and recorded its way toward giving her a complete document to hold in her lap.

The first page seemed without precedent. Below the name of the Court and the caption of the case was a statement in bold italics, followed by the signatures of all eight Judges. The statement read:

"By our ruling today, this Court intends to help avert a tragedy of global proportions, a tragedy occasioned by the total failure of effective governance."

The opinion described Hershel's participation in the murder of a defenseless Arab family that was attempting to return to their farm in 1948. The Judges then set forth details of the suicide bombing in April of 2007 by the young man, Rami Abu Mussal, that took the lives of Hershel's relatives.

The first issue the Court dealt with was whether the killings in 2007 were sufficiently connected to Hershel's war crime in 1948, such that he could properly be held to account for them. Not depending on his waiver of that defense, the Judges required the finding of a causal connection between the two events.

With biblical simplicity, they reasoned, "In all that intervening time, there was no governing authority that could have offered justice and protection. In the absence of governance, there was only violence to be expected, and violence begat violence. Revenge was as foreseeable as memory itself. We thus find a causal connection between the events of 1948 and 2007."

Anne drew a small star, lightly in pencil, to the left of the next paragraph. "Lack of effective governance is a critical concept, not only for understanding why violence became inevitable. It is the key to assessing culpability for the lawlessness, the subversion of Constitutional rights, and the changes that need to be made."

The next 150 pages reflected years of scholarship by Judge Schoft. The opinion described a list of world empires with emphasis on the Roman Empire that ended over a thousand years before and the British Empire that concluded in 1945, crushed by the weight of two World Wars.

"The latest empire, the American Empire," the Court noted, "began in earnest in 1945, when the United States was the only remaining superpower in the world, all contenders having been devastated by that last extended military conflict with Germany, Italy, and Japan."

The Court then discussed accounts of meetings among American industrialists in 1944, in which they planned the country's future after World War II. President Eisenhower, in his famous 1961 Farewell Address to the Nation, spoke about the dire results of their work. He warned that the recently formed military-industrial complex has "endangered our liberties." In that assessment, the Court said, Eisenhower was not alone. The conclusion was so obvious, the judges noted, that historians of all persuasions agreed, including C. Wright Mills, Friedrich Hayak, and George F. Kennan.

The opinion, with laser-like accuracy, Anne noted, showed how President Harry Truman had been manipulated into refusing to allow the possibility of a true world government. His failure to give control of atomic weaponry over to the United Nations and his launching of an arms race with the Soviet Union ended all hopes for effective world governance. "Thereafter," Anne read, "the United States went to war, overtly and covertly, continuously from 1945 on through to the present day."

The Judges described how the American people were deceived by brilliant public relations campaigns. The first falsely portrayed the Russians as intending to conquer the world through military means after the Second World War. The second shifted hatred of Germans to the Russians, even though victory in the Second World War was entirely bottomed on Russia's valiant defense against the Third Reich. The third propaganda campaign falsely identified independence movements throughout the world with the excesses of the Russian leader, Joseph Stalin.

After summarizing the long list of American aggressive actions (overt and covert) around the world, the Judges concluded that, "The American Empire, protected by a veto power in the Security Council of the United Nations, exercised power throughout the world beyond all limits of reason and moral constraint."

Anne could not believe how deft the Judges were in the selection of a prime example to show that the American Empire operated without civilized limits. "It was," the opinion read, "lunacy in the service of economic interests for the American government to have stirred up and armed elements of Islam to war against the Russians in Afghanistan. To have taken one of the more peaceful religions in the world into turmoil and bloodshed was an evil rarely seen in all the annals of world history. The final insult," the Court continued, "was a declaration of war by the United States against the very evil that it had created, an armed and agitated Islam. Again, more lunacy in the service of economic interests."

After Anne read that paragraph, she thought of Judge Schoft working assiduously to be accurate. She imagined him sharing drafts of the opinion with Judge Leber. And she imagined meetings with all eight of the Judges in which every detail in every paragraph needed to be verified. The process, she imagined, had to have been a historian's delight. She wished she could have been present for just some small part of that effort.

The opinion described the personal burden that Hershel carried on that night in 1948. The Judges wrote about thousands of years of stubborn, unreasonable anti-Semitism, a horrendous weight that was intensified, they said, by the Nazi occupation of Continental Europe and the Holocaust that followed. The Zionist assertion, they said, that Palestine offered a unique refuge in all the world for Jews was a palpable belief for Hershel.

They next listed, in great detail, promises made since World War I to both Arabs and Jews about hegemony in Palestine. That promise to the Jews was underscored in the recognition of the State of Israel by the President of the United States on May 14, 1948, within minutes of its Declaration of Independence.

Presidential recognition, the Judges said, was "irresponsible because it was not coupled with efforts to avoid hostilities. The British had pulled out, and the only nation in the world that had the capacity to offer troops to keep the peace while differences between Arabs and Jews could be managed was the United States.

"The fear of annihilation that Mr. Selden expected by the combined efforts of the Palestinians together with armies of the nations of Syria, Lebanon, Jordan, and Egypt was not unwarranted. So understandable was that apprehension," they said, "that it had to be taken into consideration when determining his culpability for the war crime he committed."

Anne circled the next sentence. "We hold that true culpability for Mr. Selden's actions belongs to the United States, the sole remaining superpower at the end of the Second World War, when it relegated the United Nations to a position of impotence and recognized the State of Israel without offering to send troops to act as peacekeepers so that bloodshed could have been avoided. Lawlessness in 1948," the paragraph concluded, "was not inherent in the human condition. Nor was it as a result of conditions beyond the power of the United States. In fact, the lawlessness that existed in that year was the goal that this latest superpower had in mind as it set about to use both force and stealth for gain around the world.

"The United States, a renegade nation," they actually used that word Anne said out loud, "continues operations to this day, carelessly overthrowing governments, listening to private conversations, jailing dissidents, and imposing itself in every capital of the world through trade treaties, bursts of propaganda, and threats of expulsion from an inner circle of commerce.

"Hershel Selden has been referred to as a puppet. The metaphor is accurate. He did what he could under circumstances that had been determined for him. The strings had all been held by a government that broke global promises about peace, beginning in the year 1945. His culpability was negligible compared to the United States. We accept his assertions of guilt and determine that his punishment has been satisfied through the assiduous efforts he's made to bring about justice for himself and for others."

The next paragraph made Anne shiver. "Are we not all puppets then if we fail to cut the strings that bind us and allow freedom to step forth?" The Judges went on to call upon the German government to resist the empire created by the United States. The Court would make itself available to assist with any and all efforts of the Chancellor's office, the Bundestag, and the Bundesrat to turn matters around.

"If the United Nations refuses to reconfigure itself and operate without a Security Council, Germany must consider leaving and leading other nations into a new international body, one that will create peace, bring about disarmament, and assure survival."

The Court urged recognition of the rights of people around the world to determine their own paths to attain human dignity, peace, and justice. "Currently," the decision said, "the only binding international order that exists consists of trade treaties and monetary policy organizations which mostly serve corporate and financial interests."

The Court went on: "To emphasize our position, we use the word impossible. It will be impossible to bring an end to war, control corporate excesses, and reverse policies that threaten continued habitability on this planet, as long as there is no true governance over this Earth.

"We have no recourse other than to begin anew by helping to reconfigure international governance. May that new body be, to borrow a famous phrase, of the people, by the people, and for the people. Living at an impasse, as though it were the only reality possible, is impermissible.

"Toward that end, this Court retains jurisdiction to include as litigants all persons who wish to come forward as did Mr. Selden. We will help give protection to those who wish to testify concerning war crimes, including the events surrounding September 11, 2001, and the continuous unreasonable eavesdropping that's now taking place. In addition, we retain jurisdiction to make determinations concerning resignations from the United Nations as well as resignations from the various world trade and monetary organizations. Finally, we retain jurisdiction for any rulings that might become necessary during the formation of a new international body, out of which will come true world governance. For purposes of beginning discussions of that process, we wish to call that body One World United."

Chapter 32

November winds were light that unseasonably warm afternoon. A bright sun played through the bare branches of tall trees, as Anne and Hershel walked, holding hands, on Summit Lane in the Watchung Mountains of New Jersey. They walked past the riding stables that, in the late 1950s, had been a launching area for Nike Missiles, protection against the hyped-up fear that Russian bombers carrying nuclear weapons were about to destroy America. A sign marked that historic use of the property by the United States Army.

Anne thought about how frightened she'd been back then. Her school conducted air raid drills. She dutifully ducked under the desk, picturing monsters talking a foreign language as they aimed their bombs down on good and helpless people like herself.

"Nothing from Steiner today about Judge Schoft?" she asked.

"Nothing," Hershel said. "Every day there's no bad news is a blessing."

Judge Schoft had received death threats just before the opinion was published. It was to take pressure off of him that the first page contained that unusual statement of purpose signed by the entire panel. The Judges would not let intimidation deter them from the course they had chosen.

How might the cabal, the secret government, the military industrial complex, react was a question that Anne asked herself every day? In the 1950s, they used the hyped up threat of evil emanating from Moscow to sow policies that confounded dissent. Now, the German legislature and the Chancellor's Office were taking The Puppet's Case seriously. How might those who hold power in the United States react to this unprecedented challenge?

Hershel and Anne turned right on Summit Road, a street that ran along the crest of the Watchung Mountains, and were treated to a glistening bright view of the New York City skyline. It was here that Anne went to see the smoke that came from the destruction of the Twin Towers on September 11, 2001. And she remembered being frightened again, thinking she would need protection once more, this time from odious remnants of the Ottoman Empire gone mad. That recollection of fear made Anne ask herself again, how will the owners of America act? What will they do in an effort to avoid defeat?

Hershel, after returning from Karlsruhe, received an array of communications that were forwarded from Steiner. They ranged from hate mail to messages of thanks. He carried one letter with him. It came from a young poet who lived in Haifa. The lines she wrote became imprinted upon his consciousness. With so few words, the poet captured Hershel's hope for the future. It read:

Israel is as well
A place in the heart
That the cunning
Will keep us from,
If we allow.

After looking at the skyline for a while, they walked back up Summit Road and turned left toward the stable on Summit Lane. In the distance, a black car was headed toward them. It picked up speed, but neither Anne nor Hershel took notice of it. And neither of them saw that the driver's eyes were closed, his head was pitched forward, and his hands were not on the wheel.

When the car was nearly upon them, they could see that the driver was either asleep or dead. Hershel pushed Anne with all the strength he had toward the woods on his left. The vehicle hit him square, throwing him over a hundred feet through the air and running over his body before crashing into a stand of trees.

Anne ran to Hershel's very still and bloodied body. She called his name. She kissed his face. She felt his neck for a pulse. But he was gone, and now she knew. The fight ahead might be long and difficult. "Long and difficult, I know," she said to Hershel.

Anne cradled him in her lap until police cars and an ambulance arrived. When they asked her to move away, she refused to do so unless they abided by a condition.

"Of course," one of the responders said, while the other was setting up a stretcher.

"You give this man the respect he deserves," she ordered.

"Yes. Yes. I already said of course. Of course I will."

Anne shifted her weight backward so that the responder could settle Hershel's head slowly toward the pavement.

"He's a very special soldier," she said with solemnity.

"Yes, of course."

Anne felt the scene of horror fading slightly as she floated toward Kevin and Amy who rushed over to her and hugged her. "I have a job for you," she told them.

"I know what it is," Amy said.

"Me too," Kevin responded.

"So you'll both take care of him. Make sure to tell him where he is and that I love him dearly. You'll both do that for me?"

Kevin and Amy said yes and gave Anne long hugs.

"And tell Jesus that Hershel did everything he possibly could do."

"We will. Goodbye. We love you," they echoed.

Above the three ambulances and five police cars that had gathered below, a drone the size of a small suitcase hovered. The circuit that had controlled the car from above was deactivated. The crash site was being cordoned off. Traffic was rerouted. The drone sped off, toward a van parked on a little-used runway of a private airport to the north, in Morristown.

The war has begun, Anne said quietly to herself. Those who hold the power lack all humanity. But this time, she would fight with every ounce of herself against the lies and the violence to come. "Not just Israel," she said, as the police began asking her about what had happened. "The world is a place in my heart that..."

"I'm sorry, what did you say, mam?" asked the police officer.

"Cunning bastards," Anne replied.

"Are you all right?"

"I'm fine, but you need to know something, officer. What happened here was a murder, not some accident. This is a crime scene. Did you hear me?"

"And you know that because?"

"Because my friend was the target."

"Maybe we should get you to the hospital."

"Not before I'm assured that the electrical system of that car will be checked to see if it had been tampered with so that it could have been controlled by a drone."

True to her word, Anne didn't leave the scene. And she was joined by Alan. Together, they were assured that the vehicle would be guarded and the electrical system properly examined.

Results of the examination showed that Hershel had, indeed, been murdered. Egon and Steiner put all of that relevant information into the record of The Puppet's Case.

Some fourteen thousand men and women, the world over, joined the case as additional plaintiffs within the first month. Eleven nations had begun the process of creating and becoming a part of One World United. And finally, a court, the Constitutional Court in Karlsruhe, made itself available to begin hearings that would separate truth from lies. No longer would clever propaganda go unchallenged.

Using The Puppet's Case, Judges were cutting the strings that formerly had bound humanity to the wielders of power.

One World United, Anne understood, would prevail. The people were finally, day by day, creating proper governance for themselves, for the Earth, and for the generations to come.

AFTERWORD

Ralph Waldo Emerson referred to writers as explorers. Every step, he said, is an advance into new land. The novel, *Impasse*, is an effort to take us to a place we've never experienced, an Earth on which peace prevails. Since recorded history, human affairs have been dominated by ever larger swaths of conquering empires. With environmental destruction near, that paradigm needs to be abandoned. And time is of the essence.

Impasse hones in on a war crime committed by the protagonist, Hershel Selden, in the 1948 Israel/Palestine War. He participated in the murder of an Arab family who were attempting to return to their farm. Although it's a fictional event, such things occurred in that war. Arabs who were attempting to return to their towns and villages were sometimes met with live fire.[1]

Selden's crime had ramifications. Years later, members of his family were killed in a suicide bombing near where he murdered the Arab family. Didn't Hershel's criminal act fuel the vengeance that took his own family? Why am I being treated as a war hero, he asks, when I am, in fact, responsible for the deaths of my own family?

His efforts to find justice take Hershel Selden to the Constitutional Court of the Federal Republic of Germany. Located in Karlsruhe, it's renowned, says Supreme Court Judge Ruth Bader Ginsburg, for safeguarding individuals against oppressive governments and stirred-up majorities.[2] Selden has obviously come to the right place to find answers. German criminal jurisprudence goes far beyond mere findings of guilt or innocence. Its primary goal is discovery of truth.[3]

The Court holds that Hershel Selden's responsibility is minimal compared to that of the nation states which refuse to accept any real system of order in the world. There are millions of Seldens committing similar war crimes all the time, the Justices say, because there is no order. And that portends a bleak future.

The Court goes on to find that the United Nations, dominated as it is by the latest world empire, the United States, cannot possibly bring about peace. It therefore orders the Republic of Germany to leave that body and form another, one that's capable of bringing about—finally— international accord and peace for the benefit of all the people.

Well, does *Impasse,* as Ralph Waldo Emerson said, deliver as a proper vehicle for exploration into a new land? Should the United States be seen as the stumbling block to true international governance? Are we now required to jettison the United Nations and create another, more effective body? The answer to all three questions is yes.

As characters in the novel point out, for the last hundred years American oligarchic/corporate power has attempted to destroy ideas and initiatives which might have limited profits. That conduct, protected by a veto power in the Security Council, will continue unabated, even though survival requires attention to concepts that challenge the profit-motive-uber-alles point of view.

Here's the historical record. The United States, along with fourteen foreign countries, intervened in the Russian Civil War in an effort to destroy the very idea of communism,[4] refusing a peace offer that would have confined Russia to a small area ringed by capitalist countries.[5] At home, the American government began to treat citizens whose beliefs even slightly resembled socialism or communism as criminals.[6] That destruction of the left continued and ushered in a maelstrom of politics bereft of reason to this day.[7] After WWII, the United States plunged the nations back into warfare by falsely claiming that the USSR intended to take over the world by military means.[8] And when the USSR collapsed, the United States declared war against "terrorism," a mission to benefit the military-industrial complex made possible by a false flag operation on September 11, 2001.[9]

Villainy with the power of a veto adds up to destruction and chaos. The choice is yours. I suggest that you enter new land by affirming the decision of the Constitutional Court at Karlsrue. Do it in any way you can and wherever you reside. Do it for the children because, as Dostoyevsky's Fr. Zossima pleads, they are sinless and in our care.[10]

1. Benny Morris, *1948: A History of The First Arab-Israeli War* (New Haven and London: Yale University Press, 2008), page 294.
2. Ruth Bader Ginsburg, Forward to the Third Edition of *The Constitutional Jurisprudence of the Federal Republic of Germany* by Donald P. Kommers and Russell A. Miller, Duke University Press (Durham and London, 2012).
3. Markus D. Dubber, "The Promise of German Criminal Law: A Science of Crime and Punishment," (University of Toronto, 2004), page 10, published in the Social Science Research Network.
4. W. Bruce Lincoln, *Red Victory: A History of the Russian Civil War* (New York: Simon and Schuster, 1989), pages 12 and 184.
5. Sigmund Freud and William C. Bullitt, *Thomas Woodrow Wilson: A Psychological Study* (Boston: Houghton Mifflin Company, 1966) page 253.
6. Ann Hagedorn, *Savage Peace: Hope and Fear in America 1919* (New York: Simon & Schuster) pages 430-432.
7. Ellen Schrecker, *Many are the Crimes: McCarthyism in America* (Little, Brown, and Company, 1998, pages 412-415.
8. Arnold A. Offner, *Another Such Victory: President Truman and the Cold War 1945-1953* (Stanford University Press, 2002) pages 193 and 199-202.
9. John C. Austin, "American Nightmare 2001-?," *The 9/11 Conspiracy: The Scamming of America*, ed. James H. Fetzer (Peru, Illinois: Catfeet Press, 2007) pages 1-12.
10. Fyodor Dostoyevsky, *The Brothers Karamozov* (Random House: The Modern Library, 1950) page 383.

AUTHOR BIOGRAPHY

Michael Diamond received his law degree from Rutgers University. His major focus became environmental policy when he realized that the regulatory systems that had been set up in the United States had failed.

With rates of diseases like cancer, asthma, autism, and Alzheimer's climbing steadily, Diamond was the first to call for use of the little known civil emergency provision in the US Constitution to deal effectively with the crisis. He remains preeminent in the study of that provision—the domestic violence clause in Article IV, Section 4. "Use of it," Diamond says "will unseat corporate control in the United States."

Diamond wrote *Impasse* both to entertain and make accessible to the public a true pathway to peace. The vision set forth in the novel is a new international order, one that works, finally, for the benefit of the earth and all its people.

Made in the USA
Middletown, DE
08 August 2016